TRANSFORMERS
ROBOTS IN DISGUISE

Little, Brown and Company
Hachette Book Group
1290 Avenue of the Americas, New York, NY 10104
Visit us at lb-kids.com

Little, Brown and Company is a division of Hachette Book Group, Inc. The Little, Brown name and logo are trademarks of Hachette Book Group, Inc.

The publisher is not responsible for websites (or their content) that are not owned by the publisher.

First Edition: September 2016

Transformers Robots in Disguise: Bumblebee Versus Scuzzard originally published in May 2015 by Little, Brown and Company
Transformers Robots in Disguise: Drift's Samurai Showdown originally published in September 2015 by Little, Brown and Company
Transformers Robots in Disguise: The Trials of Optimus Prime originally published in January 2016 by Little, Brown and Company

Library of Congress Control Number: 2016938006

ISBN 978-0-316-39618-9

10 9 8 7 6 5 4 3 2 1

RRD-C

Printed in the United States of America

Licensed By:

Action and
Adventure
Collection

by John Sazaklis & Steve Foxe

LITTLE, BROWN AND COMPANY
New York   Boston

Table of Contents

Sideswipe

Grimlock

Slipstream

Jetstorm

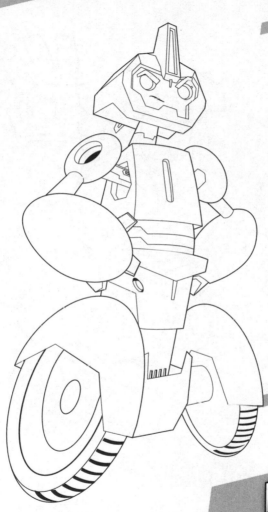

fixit

Micronus

Optimus

Bumblebee
Versus
Scuzzard

Bumblebee Versus Scuzzard

by John Sazaklis

Chapter 1

"Stop in your tracks, Decepticon!" shouts Bumblebee. "You're under arrest!"

The Autobot leader blasts his plasma cannon. The rapidly moving target leaps from side to side then somersaults over the Cybertronian lieutenant, landing behind him. The agile adversary shoves Bumblebee to the ground.

"Is that the best you got, law-bot?" taunts a familiar voice.

It is Bumblebee's teammate: the youthful, energetic, and rebellious Sideswipe.

He scowls at Bumblebee and yells, "You're scrap metal!"

Sideswipe then smiles, extends his arm, and helps his sparring partner off the ground.

"Pretty impressive," Bumblebee says. "You've got some nice moves, but the tough-bot attitude might be a bit over the top, don't you think?"

The young Autobot laughs. "You got to be a tough-bot if you want to intimidate those Decepticons, Bee."

"Thanks for the advice," Bumblebee replies. "Who's next?"

The Autobot leader scans the scrapyard that currently serves as their headquarters and training area.

Located on the outskirts of Crown City on planet Earth, the scrapyard belongs to a pair of humans: Denny Clay and his son, Russell. The Clays have befriended Bumblebee and his robot team and sometimes help them on their mission to track down and capture a number of Decepticon fugitives from the planet Cybertron.

"It is my turn, sir," calls out Strongarm. The young cadet dutifully strides over to the center of the training area.

Back on Cybertron, Strongarm was a member of the police force serving under Lieutenant Bumblebee. Now she helps serve and protect anyone or anything that may come to harm at the hands of the Autobots' evil enemies on Earth.

"Let's see if your moves are as good as mine," Sideswipe says to her. "Not everyone gets the best of Bee. But *I* did!"

"Show some respect, Sideswipe," replies Strongarm. "You may have advanced 'street smarts' back home, but you're no intellitron. Bumblebee is your commanding officer, and you should treat him as such!"

"You're right," snaps Sideswipe. "So I only have to listen to *him*. Not you!"

"Fine," huffs the police-bot. "Who says I want to waste nanocycles talking to *you* anyway?" Strongarm retorts. "I'd have to use smaller words and talk...very...slowly."

"Enough!" Bumblebee says, exasperated. "We are all on the *same* team, whether we like to admit it or not. The real foes are out there, and we need to be prepared. Something terrible is on the horizon, and by the AllSpark, I sure hope we can handle it!"

"Yes, sir," Strongarm says. "Let's continue training."

"Where are Grimlock and Drift?" Sideswipe asks.

Grimlock is a Dinobot and former Decepticon who defected to the Autobots, and Drift is an honorable bounty hunter. They're also part of Bumblebee's ragtag team.

"Drift has a free pass from today's training," Bumblebee replies. "He took the Groundbridge to an area with an allegedly high concentration of Energon. You know how he likes his solo missions."

"Yeah, Drift sure is a real-deal tough-bot," Sideswipe says. "Glad he's on our side."

Bumblebee chuckles. "I asked him to recon and report back," the leader says. "If there is Energon out there, we'll travel to the location and harvest the power source right away."

"Excellent," Strongarm cheers. "Another mission!"

"I totally understand your enthusiasm, Strongarm," Bumblebee replies. "Things have been a little quiet around here."

"Yeah, quiet until the storm hits," Sideswipe says, slamming his fist into his palm. "I'm ready for whatever the Decepticons got!"

"I have a feeling the Decepticons may be

after something as big and as powerful as the AllSpark."

Strongarm gasps. "But, sir, harnessing that kind of power could bring about unimaginable destruction!"

Bumblebee nods grimly.

Sideswipe breaks the uncomfortable silence and tries to lighten the mood. "Speaking of destruction, what's Grimlock up to?"

"He's recharging on top of a pile of old cars," a voice answers.

The Autobots turn to see Russell, their twelve-year-old human friend. "Grimlock found a nice sunny spot, and he's lying in it like a big lizard."

"Hey, Russell," Bumblebee says. "What's up?"

"Shouldn't you be at lob-ball practice?" asks Sideswipe.

Russell chuckles. "Here on Earth, it's called football."

"Oh, right," Sideswipe says, trying to remember the word. "Foot. Ball."

"We're on spring break from school," Russell continues.

"Spring break?" Strongarm asks in a puzzled voice.

"Yeah."

Suddenly, Fixit rolls into the training area from behind a dented billboard.

"Who has a spring break?" Fixit asks. "It's about time! I've been itching to repaint... repeat... repair something."

The multitasking mini-con was pilot of

the prison transport ship *Alchemor*—the same ship that crashed to Earth and let loose the Decepticon criminals aboard. Now he rounds out the rest of Team Bee as the resident handy-bot.

After the crash, Fixit developed a minor stutter, but he manages to correct his vocabulary with a quick check.

The mini-con weaves in and out between the legs of the Autobots, twitching his digits excitedly.

"No one had anything break," Bumblebee says, looking himself over. "As far as I can tell."

Russell laughs. "Spring break is another term for taking a vacation from school."

"What's a vacation?" Strongarm asks.

"It's time off," Sideswipe replies. "Like an extended holiday."

Strongarm's optics open wide with surprise. "Who would want to take time off from school?"

"Not Miss Perfect Attendance, I'm sure," Sideswipe retorts.

"Every single cycle!" Strongarm announces proudly.

"Really? I'm impressed, cadet," Bumblebee says. "That's an excellent record!"

"I know!" Strongarm beams.

Sideswipe rolls his optic sensors.

"Anyway," Russell interrupts. "My friends Hank and Butch are going away with their families for the next week and, well, I'm kind of stuck here, where nothing exciting has happened in *ages*."

The boy kicks a rock and sits on an over-turned shopping cart.

"That's not so bad," Fixit replies. "I'm stumped . . . stunned . . . stuck here all the time when all the other bots are out on missions or when they play games together."

"Every team member's duty is very impor-tant," Bumblebee explains. "Especially yours, Fixit."

Sideswipe sighs. "All right. There's only so much sappy goodness this bot can take before he gets brain rust."

He walks over and crouches near the mini-con.

"So, you *really* wanna play lob-ball with us? You got it!"

With a loud whistle, the red robot wakes up Grimlock.

"Big G!" Sideswipe hollers. "We're playing lob-ball with Fixit. Go long!

"Finally!" Grimlock exclaims as he stretches his limbs. "Something to do that involves some action!"

Fixit rubs his digits together with anticipation and excitement.

"Excellent. What's my position?"

Sideswipe smirks and picks up the mini-con.

"Ball," he says.

Then, in one deft movement, he hurls Fixit through the air straight at Grimlock.

"AAAAAAAAAH!" screams the mini-con as he becomes a tiny dot against the sky.

Bumblebee sighs and hangs his head.

"When I said we need to focus on working as a team, this is not what I had in mind."

Grimlock jumps off the pile of cars and dashes into action. Shifting into his bot mode, he grabs an old metal bathtub and scrunches it onto his head.

With his makeshift helmet secured, the Dinobot rushes toward Fixit, all the while giving a running commentary.

"This is it, ladies and gentlebots! Only mere nanocycles left in the game. Cybertron Lob-ball Legend Gridlock Grimlock sprints to catch the final pass. Will it be the winning play? Keep your optics open. You won't want to miss a thing!"

"Gridlock! Grimlock! Gridlock! Grimlock!" chants Sideswipe.

Grimlock catches Fixit, pulls him into his chest, pivots, and charges in the opposite direction. When he reaches the end of the scrapyard, he hoists Fixit high into the air.

"Grimlock wins the game for Team Bee! The crowd goes wild!"

Sideswipe turns on his car radio speakers and blasts a bass-heavy techno sports jam.

"Go, Grimlock, it's your botday!" he sings, while dancing to the beat.

Caught up in the excitement, Grimlock moves to spike Fixit into the ground as if he were a real football!

"Grimlock, *no*!" Strongarm shouts.

Quick as a flash, she and Bumblebee shift into their vehicle modes and rush to the rescue.

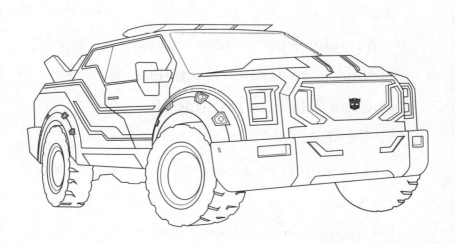

They corner Grimlock just as he spikes the mini-con. Bumblebee's tires screech and squeal and kick up dirt as he pulls a 180-degree turn. The yellow sports car pops his trunk, and Fixit lands safely inside.

Bumblebee then changes back into bot mode and cradles the mini-con.

Fixit's gears are rattling. "I think that's enough feet...feed...fieldwork for one day. Thanks."

As Bumblebee readies himself to scold Grimlock, Sideswipe blindsides him and snatches Fixit from his arms.

"INTERCEPTION!" shouts Sideswipe, and he sprints away toward the other end of the yard.

Grimlock bounds after him.

Bumblebee throws up his hands and looks at the sky. When he feels troubled, he seeks guidance from his fallen hero, Optimus Prime.

"Optimus, if you can hear me, please give me a sign. Anything that will—aha!"

A shiny object glints in the sunlight, catching Bumblebee's attention.

For a moment, the Autobot sees the reflection of Optimus Prime, but it is gone as soon as it appeared.

It is that same object that gives Bumblebee an idea. Shifting into vehicle mode, he speeds past the other Autobots and reaches the end of the scrapyard first. He switches back and climbs inside a truck with a hydraulic magnet attached. Bumblebee pulls down on a large lever, and the machine whirs to life. The hydraulic arm drops toward the ground—at the same exact moment that Grimlock and Sideswipe race by underneath!

CLANG!

CLANG!

The robots are yanked off their feet and right onto the magnet.

"AAH!" they shout.

Sideswipe freaks out and drops Fixit, but Strongarm is there to catch him.

The mini-con's optic sensors are swirling wildly. He is seeing double.

"Strongarm, how long have you had a sitter...a sitar...a sister?" he asks. "Are you twigs...twits...twins? She looks just like you! Pleasure to meet you, my dear!"

Fixit bows his head and passes out.

"Hey, what's the big idea?" Sideswipe hollers.

"Game over," Bumblebee says sternly.

Grimlock looks down and sees his feet dangling high above the yard.

"I can fly!" he cheers.

Bumblebee pulls the lever again, deactivating the magnet, and releases his fellow Autobots onto the ground below.

CRASH!

Suddenly, Denny Clay comes running into the scrapyard. He is flustered and gasping for breath.

"Dad, is everything okay?" Russell asks.

"You'll never guess what happened!" Denny blurts out.

"What is it?"

"It's something that's going to change our lives forever!"

Russell looks at the robots and says, "What could possibly change our lives *more* than our new houseguests?"

"It's not kittens, is it?" Grimlock asks warily.

The Dinobot has an incredible fear of cats but tries not to let it show.

"I think I hear Drift calling me. I'll go see what he wants."

The Dinobot runs away to the other side of the scrapyard, much to the bewilderment of his teammates.

Denny sits down to catch his breath. He is huffing and puffing and wheezing.

A revived Fixit rolls over and scans him.

"I'm not familiar with organic biology, but it appears that Denny Clay is running on fumes. Does he need more fuel? I have my grandbot's home remedy right here in the holo-scroll!"

Fixit rolls away into the command center.

After what seems like an eternity for the anxious group, Denny finally catches his breath and says, "An old friend of mine called up to say he's got two amazing items for sale. You'll never guess! Okay, I'll tell you. Vintage pinball machines!"

Russell, disappointed, slumps his shoulders. "Oh. More junk."

"Hey, these things are *super* rare!" Denny says excitedly. "Not exactly in working order, but repairing them will give us something to do together."

"Pardon us for asking," Bumblebee interrupts, "but what are pinball machines? Are they good or bad?"

"Do they shoot pins?" Strongarm asks.

"Ha, no!" Denny says with a laugh. "They're old-fashioned coin-operated arcade games."

"Oooh, games!" Sideswipe says.

"Don't get too excited," Russell responds.

"They're ancient history. Just like everything else in this place."

Denny tries to cheer up his son. "Come on, Rusty. We'll take a little road trip together. It'll be a blast and a half! Things seem to be quiet here."

"Your father is right," Bumblebee says. "I'm confident we can manage for a while without you. Go and enjoy yourselves."

"Fine," Russell says. Then he whispers to Sideswipe. "Call us back immediately if something exciting happens, so I don't die of boredom."

"You got it, dude."

As Denny and Russell head inside to prepare for their trip, the Autobots disperse throughout the yard.

Grimlock returns with a brave face. "Hey, I don't think that was Drift calling me after all!" he says with a chuckle.

Seeing that he is alone, a wave of panic grips the Dinobot.

"Oh no!" He gulps. "It *was* kittens!"

Chapter 3

"All aboard!" Denny says as he climbs into his pickup truck.

Russell climbs into the passenger seat and buckles himself in. His father is elated.

"I can't wait to get my hands on those fantastic fixer-uppers!"

"So, where are we headed exactly?"

"My old high school buddy Doug Castillo owns an arcade near the amusement park. Doug's Den is the name, and he's got *all* the old-school video games. I always wanted to take you there when you were younger but never got the chance."

As Denny loses himself in a wave of nostalgia, Russell falls silent and stares out the window. It's true his father was not around much when he was growing up. Now, with his mom traveling in Europe, Russell is spending a lot more time with his dad.

It was not long after Russell moved to the scrapyard, or, as his father calls it, the "vintage salvage depot for the discriminating nostalgist," that the Autobots literally crashlanded into their lives.

Russell watches the trees whiz by and wonders how vast the universe must be if alien robots really exist on other planets. Especially when these robots are sentient beings with the ability to reconfigure their alien anatomy into that of vehicles or animals while battling one another right outside his very home.

The pickup continues over the bridge leading into the city. Denny rolls down the windows and turns on the radio. A summer-like beach-rock tune fills the air.

Denny sighs happily. "It's good to get away!"

Meanwhile, underneath the bridge in a murky marsh, a large metallic object glints in the sun. Part of it is submerged in water, and most of the exterior is damaged.

When the *Alchemor* crashed to Earth, a number of prison cells known as stasis pods were scattered across the surrounding area.

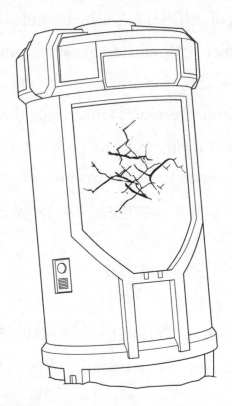

Those pods housed Cybertron's most violent criminals—Decepticons.

Unfortunately, some of them had escaped their pods, and it is Bumblebee's mission to round up the rogues.

This particular pod starts to shift and rattle as the prisoner stirs within.

CRACK.

CRACK.

CRACK.

A sharp, pointed beak pecks at the surface, as if hatching an egg, until it finally breaks through the stasis pod.

SKRAAAACK!

An oversized, rust-colored vulturish Decepticon emerges!

Stretching his long neck and wings, the

creature steps, blinking, into the sun. It scours the terrain for food.

"I HUNGER!" he screeches.

His raspy, grainy voice startles a nearby bullfrog, which leaps into the water.

Following the movement, the Decepticon stabs at the water with his beak and pulls out a soggy rubber boot.

"Meh!" he exclaims in disgust and flings it aside. "What is this? Where *am* I?" He turns his head from side to side, observing his surroundings.

"This is not Cybertron. We must have landed on another, far inferior planet."

Then he spots a discarded tin can. "Is that the best sustenance this ragged rock has to offer?" he squawks.

He pinches the can with his beak and swallows it in one gulp.

Suddenly, the Decepticon feels a wonderful sensation. His body ripples with energy. It grows bigger and more menacing.

"Hmm, this rock may have something to offer me after all!"

Russell and his father finally arrive at the amusement park and drive around to where Doug's Den is located.

A man with glasses and a ponytail is waiting for them with a big grin on his face. Russell guesses that it is Doug.

"Denny, you ol' sea dog!" Doug hollers

as Russell and his dad exit the pickup. He squeezes Denny in a bear hug that lifts him off the ground.

"Dougie, you haven't changed a bit. I want you to meet my son, Rusty."

The boy shakes Doug's hand and says, "It's Russell, actually."

"And I'm Doug," the man says with a wink. "Come on in, I'll show you around!"

Russell and his father walk through the arcade, looking at all the classic video games. There is one where a yellow circle with a mouth eats white dots while running from multicolored ghosts. Another one stars a short plumber with a mustache that has to save a princess.

"*Wow!* This is awesome!" Denny gushes. "What do you think, Rusty?"

"I think it's cool…if not a little *old*."

"Russell, apologize!" his father scolds.

Doug laughs. "No offense taken. The boy's right. Kids today have portable, digital, highly advanced technology in the palm of their hands. Why would they waste their time with these clunky old dinosaurs?"

"You don't need to tell *me* about clunky dinosaurs," Denny says. He looks at Russell with a gleam in his eye. Russell smiles knowingly.

"I might as well shut this place down or turn it into a museum," Doug continues. "I'll charge people to come in and hear me say,

'The first coin-operated pinball machine was introduced in 1931.'"

Denny brightens. "And speaking of pinball machines . . ."

"Oh, yes! Right this way."

The group circles around back to the loading dock, where two time-ravaged pinball machines stand wrapped in plastic.

Russell can see the intricate illustrations painted on the back panels of each game. They are of a grizzled adventurer wearing a leather jacket and brown fedora. In one, he is riding a horse into the mouth of a cave shaped like a skull. In the other, he swings on a rope over a pit of cobras surrounded by flames.

Hmm, maybe these things aren't so boring after all, Russell thinks.

About half an hour later, after loading their truck and bidding Doug farewell, the duo is back on the road again.

"I can't wait to tinker with them," Denny says. "Maybe even put some of that Autobot tech in 'em. Make 'em outta this world!"

Rusty smiles. That turned out to be a fun little adventure after all.

When they reach the bridge, Denny slams on the brakes.

There appears to be a traffic jam, with several bystanders looking over the side of the bridge.

Suddenly, a screeching creature swoops up into the air.

"Is that a hawk?" Russell asks.

"It looks more like a vulture," Denny says,

his face puzzled. "We don't have many in these parts, though."

Just as suddenly, the winged beast dives and lands on the hood of the pickup, denting it under his massive weight.

CRUNCH!

Denny and Russell see the Decepticon logo on the vulture's gleaming metallic hide.

"Wish we had some Autobot tech with us right now!" Russell yells.

Chapter 4

SCREEEEEECH!

The sound of metal scraping metal is ear piercing as the Decepticon digs his claws into the hood of Denny's pickup truck.

"A prisoner has escaped!" Russell cries.

"Rusty, look out!" shouts Denny.

The vulture pecks at the glass with his giant

beak. Thin cracks creep across the windshield in a spiderweb pattern.

"We gotta call Bumblebee!" yells Russell.

"First, we gotta get this thing away from the people," replies Denny. He wrenches the wheel to the left, causing the pickup to go off the road and into the woods.

The Decepticon hisses in surprise and digs his talons in deeper to maintain a grip on the hood. Then he glares at Denny.

"We're taking the scenic route, you big buzzard," Denny says.

Rusty fumbles for the CB radio on the truck's dashboard. Once he pries it loose, he clicks on the receiver to open a connection.

The pickup's tires bump along the uneven

terrain, jostling Russell. He drops the radio, and it slides under his seat.

Denny shouts a warning as the Decepticon rears his head back for another attack. "Get down and cover your head!"

The vulture stabs at the glass again, this time penetrating it with his beak.

SHUNK!

"AAAH!"

Denny screams and reflexively turns on the windshield wipers. They begin swishing from side to side, momentarily hypnotizing the rampaging robot.

Screeching with annoyance, the Decepticon chomps down and rips them off. He chews them but finds them unsatisfactory.

"BLEH!" he yells, spitting them out. Then he turns to attack again. The windshield will not withstand another hit.

Denny uses his wits and—in a last-ditch effort—squirts the bad birdbot with wiper fluid.

SQUIRRRT!

The liquid coats the vulture's face, blinding him. Flailing his wings, he loses balance and lurches backward.

Denny cuts the wheel one more time,

causing the truck to swerve in a complete circle. The Decepticon tumbles off the hood, claws at the air, and slams into a nearby tree trunk.

BAM!

Unfortunately, one of the pinball machines is jarred loose and falls out and onto the ground. The glass display shatters into a million pieces. The metal gears and ball bearings roll over the grass, glinting and shimmering under the sun.

This catches the vulture's attention, and he descends upon the arcade game, rending it apart. The priceless pinball machine is now nothing more than a worthless chew toy.

"Oh, man!" Denny laments, looking over his shoulder.

Without a moment to lose, he slams on the gas, and the pickup truck speeds off toward the scrapyard.

Russell finally gets his hands on the CB radio and tries to contact the command center.

"There's no answer, Dad," he says.

Denny gulps and tries not to look worried in front of his son. He wipes the sweat off his brow with the back of his hand.

"Do you think our friends are in trouble?" Russell asks.

"Only one way to find out," replies Denny. "We're almost there."

Father and son ride the rest of the way in silence, both wondering what will be the outcome of this Decepticon disaster.

Chapter 5

When Russell and Denny arrive, they jump out of the truck and rush into the scrapyard, only to find it eerily quiet.

"Where is everyone?" Russell asks.

"Let's hope they didn't get carried away," Denny says.

"Dad!" Russell says.

With his father, the young boy runs up and down the aisles of piled junk, calling out the names of their friends.

Suddenly, there is a loud crash and crunching of metal followed by painful grunts and sounds of a struggle.

"Oh no!" Russell exclaims. "That sounds like trouble to me!"

The humans sprint through the mazelike scrapyard until they discover the source of the commotion.

There, in a clearing between the busted lawn mowers and a broken tractor, is an Autobot pileup.

Sideswipe is sprawled out on the bottom.

Lying on top of him are Bumblebee, then Strongarm, and finally Grimlock.

They look exhausted and defeated. Russell notices that the robots are barely moving.

"Our friends picked the wrong time to shut down," Denny says. "Now what are we going to do?"

Rusty cups his hands around his mouth and shouts. "HELP!"

The Autobots stir and turn toward the boy.

"Welcome back!" Sideswipe says cheerily from the bottom of the pile.

The robots climb off one another and help Sideswipe to his feet. Clutched close to his chest is a large concrete wrecking ball.

"We finally played a proper game of

lob-ball," he says. "And this ball is *much* better than Fixit!"

"I concur," says the mini-con, scurrying out from behind a trash can.

"See?" Sideswipe says. "Now I can do *this*!"

With one swift motion, he spikes the wrecking ball into the ground, lifting a cloud of dust and debris.

Bumblebee walks over and asks, "How was your trip?"

"Terrible!" Russell exclaims. "While you guys were running around, *we* were running for our lives!"

"What happened?" Strongarm asks.

"We were attacked by a flying Decepticon," Denny tells the group.

Stunned, the Autobots look at one another.

Without a moment to lose, they shift into their vehicle modes.

Bumblebee becomes a sleek yellow sports car and scoops up Denny into his cab.

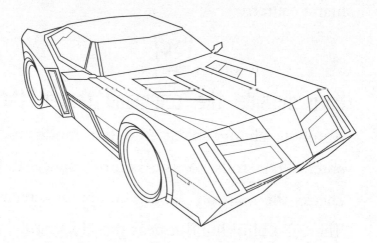

Sideswipe has the flashier and shinier appearance of a red sports car and takes Russell in tow.

Strongarm prides herself in her identity as a police sport-utility vehicle.

Fixit and Grimlock follow along in their bot modes because they do not have secret vehicle appearances to change into.

Together they all zoom back to the command center.

Once outside the command center, the

Autobots change back into bot mode and enter. Fixit rolls to the control panel and checks the map on the big computer screen. There is a blinking dot near their location.

"It would appear that there is another Decepticon on the loon...loop...loose," he says.

"You're not far off," Denny replies. "This creature *was* birdlike."

"He has razor-sharp claws and a beak and wings!" Rusty adds. "He almost made a meal out of the pickup!"

Fixit clacks away on the keyboard, calling up all known flying Decepticons on the *Alchemor*'s manifest. A few seconds later, several images appear on the holo-scroll.

Rusty and Denny point at their assailant simultaneously.

"That one!" they shout.

"His name is Scuzzard," Bumblebee reads. "And he is a Scavengebot. His abilities are similar to those of a Chompozoid."

"Our enemy Underbite is a Chompozoid, remember?" Strongarm adds. "When these Decepticons consume metal, it supercharges their bodies until they become unstoppable."

"Scavengebots have the compulsion to rend everything apart before they consume it. Most of them are pretty harmless and feast on scrap metal," explains Bumblebee. "Not Scuzzard, though."

"Hmm, I seem to remember his case," Strongarm says. "He was arrested for laying waste to a good part of Kaon's industrial area. It took an entire squadron of the capital's police force to detain and contain him!"

Denny spoke up. "This creature was about to destroy the bridge before he set his sights on us. Made a meal out of one of my poor pinball machines, too."

"So what's the plan, sir?" Strongarm asks.

"Good question," Bumblebee replies. "We need to lure the predator away from civilians, get him into a secluded area, and subdue him as quickly as possible."

"Finally!" Sideswipe says. "Just what I needed to flex my pistons!"

Bumblebee smiles. "You've given me an idea, Sideswipe. We'll send *you* out as a decoy."

"Wait, what?" replies the young Autobot. "That is a *bad* idea."

"Not really," adds Strongarm. "You're red,

shiny, and quick to catch attention. Perfect bait!"

"And you're fast," concludes Bumblebee.

Sideswipe tries to protest, but he agrees with everything his teammates have said.

"You're right," he says. "I make Decepticon hunting look *good*."

The hotshot Autobot admires his own reflection in the mirror of an old vanity nearby.

Strongarm aims her blaster and pulverizes the piece of furniture.

"Eek!" Grimlock shrieks. "That's seven cycles of bad luck!"

"Get *over* yourself," Strongarm says to Sideswipe.

"*You* get over *your*self!" Sideswipe retorts.

"Let's get this mission over with, please," Bumblebee interrupts. Then he doles out orders to the rest of the team. "Fixit, send us Scuzzard's coordinates."

As the mini-con complies, Russell and Denny consult the map.

"Hmm, that buzzardbot seems to have flown into town and is circling the area above my buddy's arcade," Denny observes.

"You have to move fast before he attacks!" Russell says.

"There's a mile of deserted road in the forest leading back here," Denny tells Bumblebee. "It's a longer route, but you can avoid the bridge and being seen by humans."

"Thank you," Bumblebee says. Then he turns to Sideswipe.

"You will get Scuzzard's attention and lure him back to the deserted road. Strongarm and I will be waiting to form a triangulation and trap him with our neo-forges."

"What about me?" asks Grimlock.

"You will stay here. These Decepticons are unpredictable. If any more of them appear, we will need you as one of our last defenses here at the base."

Forlorn, Grimlock hangs his head.

"Okay, team," says Bumblebee. "Let's cruise down to bruisetown!"

The Autobots stand still and stare at their leader. His attempts at a trademark rallying cry have been less than successful since they've arrived on Earth.

Sideswipe smiles. "How 'bout we just rock and roll?"

Bumblebee sighs. "Yeah, we can do that, too."

Quick as a flash, Sideswipe, Strongarm, and Bumblebee shift into vehicle mode and zoom out of the scrapyard.

Speeding through the forest, the Autobots trace Russell and Denny's trail to the old arcade. Their radar screens blip faster and louder, indicating that the Decepticon is near.

Bumblebee and Strongarm fall back and disappear behind a thicket of trees. They lie in wait, and Sideswipe puts his part of the plan into action.

In the distance, the red sports car sees a dark shape in the sky circling Doug's Den. At that moment, the back door opens and Doug himself exits the building. He is carrying a trash can, which he empties into a shiny metal Dumpster. Then he reenters the arcade.

Once the coast is clear, Scuzzard dives straight down and lands on the Dumpster, scattering garbage everywhere. He folds his massive wings behind him and proceeds to take giant bites out of the metal with his beak.

Sideswipe watches as the Decepticon devours the Dumpster. With each chomp, a light shimmers over his body, and Scuzzard grows larger in size. He squawks with evil glee and continues his meal.

From across the street, the Autobot steels himself and drives into the empty parking lot of the arcade.

He revs his engine.

VROOOM! VROOOM!

Scuzzard is so engrossed, he does not notice the vehicle behind him.

Exasperated, Sideswipe honks his horn impatiently, startling the escaped convict.

BEEEEEEEEEP!

Scuzzard chokes and coughs up bits of chewed metal, which land and skitter away on the asphalt.

"ACK!" He gasps. "Can't a bot eat in peace? I haven't had a decent meal in five cycles!"

Sideswipe honks again.

BEEEEEEEEEP!

Scuzzard whirls around to find a fire-engine red sports car made of delicious metal. "Well, well," he says, cocking his head. "Now, *that* looks like a decent meal!" Scuzzard stretches his wings and leaps toward Sideswipe.

The Autobot peels back in reverse, kicking up gravel, and pulls a 180-degree turn. Then he burns rubber right out of the parking lot.

"Sideswipe to Team Bee," the hero calls into his radio. "The birdbot has flown the coop…and he's coming right at me!"

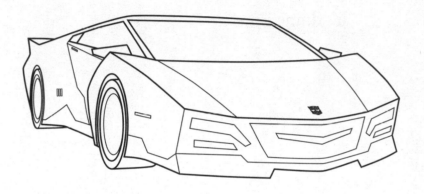

"Perfect," Bumblebee responds. "Now lead him to us!"

Scuzzard watches as his savory snack races away.

"I love it when they play hard to eat," he says to himself.

The Decepticon soars high into the air for an aerial view of Sideswipe. Once the Autobot is in his sights, Scuzzard swoops down to attack.

"It's dinnertime!"

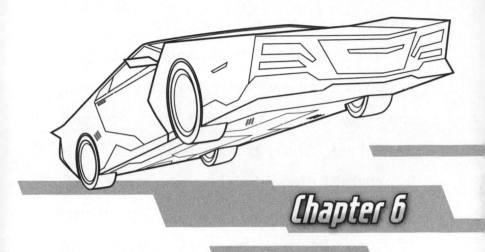

Chapter 6

Sideswipe senses his attacker gaining on him, and he barrels off the main highway and into the nearby forest. This causes Scuzzard to lose his visual on the Autobot.

The Decepticon slows his descent and peers through the treetops. Every couple of seconds, Sideswipe's red body becomes visible amid the lush green foliage.

"These peculiar organic objects may provide you temporary cover, my tender morsel, but your brightness betrays you," Scuzzard says aloud. "You're as good as digested!"

Scuzzard dives into the trees in one swift motion. His blunt body savagely rips its way through the thick branches, tearing them apart as if they were made of paper.

Sideswipe is inches away from the razor-sharp talons of his airborne adversary. He slams on the brakes and comes to a screeching halt. Scuzzard passes right over him, grazing the Autobot with his claws.

"Hey, watch the paint job, you big slag-heap!" Sideswipe shouts.

Scuzzard is slightly taken aback by the talking vehicle.

"Hmm, looks like my next meal is more than meets the eye," he says, squinting.

Sideswipe drives into a clearing and switches into his bot mode.

"If there's even the tiniest scratch on me, you'll be eating liquid fuel for a cycle!"

"It appears there's an Autobot among us," the Decepticon hisses.

Scuzzard lands and folds his wings. Then he extends to his full height, towering over Sideswipe.

The young hero had not realized how much bigger the Decepticon was up close. From afar, he seemed like a puny and easy enough challenge.

"Mama-bot told me not to play with my food, but tearing you apart is going to be *fun!*" Scuzzard gloats.

He slowly advances toward Sideswipe. The hotheaded Autobot is starting to lose his cool. He whispers into his communicator.

"Hey, guys? I could really use some backup right about now."

"We're trying to find you," Bumblebee responds.

Strongarm pipes in. "If you had stayed on course and met at the rendezvous point, this wouldn't be an issue."

Sideswipe quickly glances around. Strongarm is right. He is in the wrong part of the woods. He must have lost his way trying to outrun the Decepticon. Scuzzard sharpens his bladed fingertips against one another. The metal sparks and shrieks, causing Sideswipe to wince.

"This will not be quick, Autobot," rasps the criminal.

"Quick is what I do best," Sideswipe replies, and he turns to hightail it out of the clearing.

Just as quickly, Scuzzard pounces. He hits the Autobot square in the back, pinning him to the ground. Sinking into the dirt, Sideswipe struggles under the massive weight of the Decepticon.

"You're barely an appetizer!" Scuzzard says.

"You don't wanna to eat me," grunts Sideswipe. "I'll just get stuck in your intake valve."

"On the contrary," replies Scuzzard. "Since

my incarceration, I've built up quite an appetite."

"Then eat this!" Sideswipe yells.

He grabs a fistful of mud and hurls it at Scuzzard's face.

The Decepticon reels back.

Sideswipe rolls onto his feet.

"What is this?" spits Scuzzard. "It's vile!"

Thinking quickly, Sideswipe says, "It's a very toxic and poisonous Earth element. It will instantly deactivate you!"

Scuzzard falls to his knees and chokes.

"Curse you, Autobot!" he gasps.

Sideswipe can't believe his good fortune.

The bigger they are, the dumber they are, he thinks.

Quickly shifting into his vehicle form, Sideswipe drives farther into the forest to look for his friends.

A yellow blur blows right past him and Sideswipe swerves to follow. "Bumblebee!" he cries.

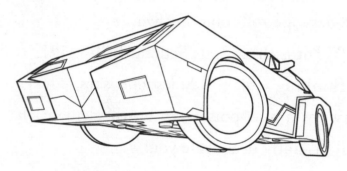

The team leader reverses and idles up next to the sports car.

Strongarm, in her police cruiser form, rolls up seconds later.

"What is the status report?" she asks.

"And where is the Decepticon?" adds Bumblebee.

As Sideswipe prepares to tell his tale, a dark shadow swoops by overhead.

SCREEECH!

"Heads up!" Strongarm warns.

The vulturish Decepticon descends upon the red sports car, landing on the roof.

"Nice try, slick," Scuzzard says, folding his wings. "You had me going for a nanocycle, but I'm still active. Only now, I'm angry!"

He rakes his sharp talons across the young hero, causing Sideswipe to yelp in pain.

Bumblebee and Strongarm surround Sideswipe and Scuzzard.

"Let me guess," the villain says. "More Autobots in disguise?"

"You got that right, criminal!" Strongarm shouts.

She shifts into her bot mode, as does Bumblebee.

"You are under arrest by order of the Cybertronian Police Force!" he says.

"*Ha!*" rasps Scuzzard. "Don't make me laugh, law-bot. We're not on Cybertron anymore!"

Scuzzard lunges at the heroes, extending his bladed wings. Bumblebee and Strongarm backflip with ease out of the criminal's razor-sharp reach. The Decepticon lands with a thud.

With his body and pride wounded, Sideswipe drives behind a row of trees and hides. He changes back into bot mode.

Bumblebee and Strongarm are ready for battle. They produce their plasma cannons and aim them at the Decepticon.

"Fire!" Bumblebee commands.

CHOOM! CHOOM!

The laser beams whiz past the vulture. He evades the blasts by soaring into the air.

"I'm just as equipped as you are," says Scuzzard as he fires a series of bladed missiles from his wings.

FWIP! FWIP! FWIP!

"Aerial assault!" Strongarm cries.

The knifelike projectiles slice through the air, stabbing everything in their path.

Bumblebee and Strongarm run for cover, but one of the bladed darts nicks Bumblebee on the leg. He stumbles and falls.

"ARGH!"

Strongarm aims her blaster from behind a tree and fires at the birdbot.

ZAP!

The energy burst catches Scuzzard square in the chest.

"Direct hit!" she cheers.

As Scuzzard falls back, he unleashes another volley of missiles.

Strongarm dives for cover as the projectiles splinter the trunk above her head. The last bladed dart bounces off her shoulder.

"Yowch!"

She spins around, reeling from the hit, and lands on her back.

Scuzzard reconfigures himself into his

large, intimidating robot form and saunters over.

He picks Strongarm up in a tight grip and holds her high above the ground. Wincing with pain, she kicks at her assailant but to no avail.

With the cadet in tow, Scuzzard walks over to her limping lieutenant and prepares to pound him into the ground with his gigantic foot.

"Just my luck," hisses Scuzzard. "I've come across an all-you-can-eat buffet!"

Chapter 7

From his hiding place, Sideswipe musters up the courage and rushes to the rescue, spiriting Bumblebee away from imminent bashing in the nick of time!

The young Autobot deposits the wounded leader against a thick tree trunk.

"I'm so sorry!" Sideswipe cries. "This is all my fault! I botched the plan!"

"We can't worry about that now," grunts Bumblebee. "I need you to focus on a *new* plan!"

Bumblebee aims the plasma cannon at his wounded leg. He sets the blaster to emit an extremely fine laser beam and mends the gash in his plating.

"Whoa," Sideswipe exclaims. "You *are* a tough-bot, Bee!"

The young Autobot is thoroughly impressed with his sometimes stodgy leader. *Maybe Strongarm is right to look up to him,* he thinks.

"Oh no! Strongarm!"

Sideswipe peeks out from behind a tree to see his teammate struggling in Scuzzard's clutches.

"Time to put my moves to good use again," Sideswipe says.

He jumps onto the nearest tree branch with ninja-like stealth and speed. He zigzags from one to the next until he disappears into the leaves above.

Ignoring his pain, Bumblebee speaks into his communicator.

"Strongarm, what is your status?"

"Oh, I'm just hanging around!" she says gruffly.

"If Strongarm is making jokes, we must *really* be in trouble!" Sideswipe quips.

"Focus, everybot. Sideswipe will be dropping in unexpectedly. Strongarm, disengage!"

"Yes, sir!"

Strongarm shifts into vehicle mode, causing Scuzzard to loosen his grip. She pops her hood, catching him on the beak with the full force of an uppercut.

BAM!

Scuzzard's head snaps back, and he drops the police SUV.

The deranged Decepticon changes into his bird form and flies up into the air. Before he can escape, Sideswipe propels himself from within the treetops and lands on top of Scuzzard.

They spiral back onto the ground, and the Autobot drills Scuzzard beakfirst into the dirt.

Before the Decepticon can recover,

Sideswipe shifts into his vehicle form and drives into Scuzzard, hitting the Decepticon with his bumper and smashing him hard against a tree.

Scuzzard drops to the ground, wheezing and hacking.

Sideswipe is mad at Scuzzard for hurting his friends as well as at himself for putting them in danger. He revs his engine and prepares to strike again. His tires spatter dirt into the air.

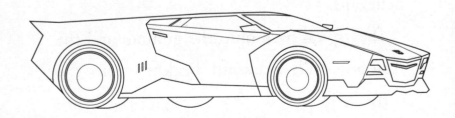

Bumblebee sternly shouts at the red sports car. "Throttle back, Sideswipe. The battle is over."

Sideswipe pulls back and shifts into his bot mode. He stands aside so that Bumblebee and Strongarm, now in bot form, can deploy their neo-forges.

Combining their forces, the heroes trap the Scavengebot in a glowing net of paralyzing energy.

"You mess with Team Bee, you're gonna get stung!" Sideswipe growls.

Scuzzard thrashes against his bonds. "Look at the brave little Autobot now. I've seen how scared you really are."

Sideswipe takes a step back as Bumblebee

and Strongarm tighten their grip on the villain.

"Before this day is done, I am going to feast on all of you!" Scuzzard sneers.

"Ugh, creepy!" Strongarm says with a shudder.

Scuzzard snaps his beak at her.

SNAP!

"Permission to treat the perpetrator as hostile, lieutenant?" she asks Bumblebee.

Before her commanding officer can answer, Strongarm judo-chops the vulture, knocking him out.

KA-POW!

"Wow," Sideswipe says, coming to a slow realization. "Strong. Arm. Now I get it!"

Strongarm lets out an unexpected laugh and quickly regains her composure.

Bumblebee puts his arms around his teammates. "If you want respect, you have to be the first to give it," he says. "How else will we succeed as a team?"

Sideswipe and Strongarm exchange glances. Their leader is right.

"Let's get back to the command center," Bumblebee says.

Back at the scrapyard, Russell and Denny are repairing the pinball machine inside Denny's garage.

Fixit rolls in and says, "I am very interested in seeing your workstop . . . chop . . . shop!"

"Come in!" Denny says with a big smile. He motions his arm in a grand sweeping gesture. "Welcome to my sanctuary!"

Fixit turns in a complete circle, taking in his new surroundings. There are several benches and shelves completely covered with numerous pieces of hardware and items in various stages of repair.

"It just looks like more of the scrapyard," Fixit says.

"That's what *I* keep telling him," Russell replies.

As Denny tinkers with his tools, he wipes the sweat off his brow.

Fixit focuses his ocular sensors onto Denny's perspiration.

"It appears you are losing fluids, Denny

Clay," Fixit says. "Perhaps one of your pipe valves has sprung a leak?"

Grimlock squeezes his massive frame into the garage.

"We just got word from Bumblebee," the Dinobot announces. "They captured the Decepticon! Whoo-hoo!"

Grimlock starts dancing, and the rumbling vibrations rattle the delicate pinball machine. The legs start to wobble and pop off one by one.

"I think there may be one too many Dino-bots in my sanctuary," Denny whispers to Russell.

"*Dad*, what am I supposed to do with him?" Russell asks. "It's not like I can take him for a walk or a run at the dog park."

"Exercise is a wonderful idea," Denny says, tousling Russell's hair. "Why don't you practice throwing a few passes? I'm sure Gridlock Grimlock is up for it."

Russell stares at his father, who continues tinkering with the pinball machine.

"Did someone call upon the lob-ball legend?" Fixit asks.

The Dinobot perks up. He reconfigures himself into bot mode and cries, "GAME ON!"

Grimlock picks up Fixit in the palm of his hand.

"Release me at once," Fixit demands.

"No, Grimlock," Denny responds with a smile. "I meant you and Rusty could throw around the old pigskin."

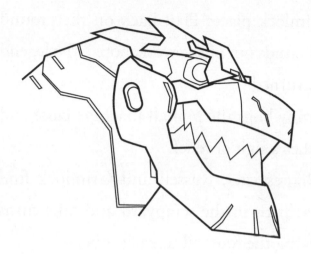

"Pigskin!" says Grimlock. "Is that another Decepticon? Let me at 'im!"

"Yes," begs the beleaguered Fixit. "Throw *him* around for a change!"

"No, no, no," Russell says, shaking his head. "Pigskin is another term for a football!"

"Ah, yes," Fixit replies. "The spheroid that is used to play your Earth sport of the same name."

Grimlock places Fixit back on the ground and bounds out of the workshop. "The legend has returned!"

Denny hugs the pinball machine close and breathes a sigh of relief.

Minutes later, Russell and Grimlock find a clear path in the scrapyard and take turns throwing the football to each other.

Russell rears back and releases the ball, spiraling it through the air at immense speed. Grimlock sprints, pushing his massive robot form to its limit, and dives to catch the football. He snatches the ball out of the air.

Unfortunately, Grimlock's rapid movement makes him an unstoppable force. He lands hard and skids uncontrollably—right into the command center!

SMASH!

CRASH!

Russell watches helplessly as the events seem to unfold in slow motion.

Grimlock bashes into one of the stasis pods, cracking the surface. The chamber tips over and breaks upon impact.

A loud hissing sound comes from within, and a sharp metallic claw scrapes away at the debris. Russell runs as fast as he can to the workshop.

"*Dad!* Fixit!" he yells. "HELP!"

Grimlock groans as he lifts his battered form onto his feet. He turns around to see the shimmering black figure of their old Decepticon nemesis—Filch!

The Corvicon slinks out of the chamber

and stretches her robot limbs while emitting
a high-pitched shriek.

"I'M FREE!"

Then she flaps her wings and takes flight.

Grimlock watches the prisoner escape.

"Oh, scrap!" he whispers.

Chapter 8

The trek back to the command center
through the forest is long and winding. The
Autobots created this path so they could travel
unobserved by humans.

Bumblebee, Sideswipe, and Strongarm take
turns carrying the unconscious form of Scuzzard. Everybot is lost in thought.

Bumblebee contemplates how the members of this motley crew of his need more field training and how they cannot rely on dumb luck to accomplish their missions.

As if reading Bumblebee's mind, Sideswipe breaks the silence.

"I want to apologize again about what happened back there," the young Autobot says. "I messed things up."

"It's all right, Sideswipe," Bumblebee says. "Any one of us could have gotten lost on this unfamiliar terrain."

"Not only that," Sideswipe says. "I'm mad at myself about being scared and running off. That's not like me. I'm tougher than that. Stronger than that!"

"Toughness is not a sign of strength," Strongarm says.

"Strongarm is right," Bumblebee adds. "You're very good at what you do, and we are all still learning how to work as a team."

Suddenly, a message crackles in through his audio receptors. Bumblebee can barely make out what it is, but he knows it's coming from the command center.

"ZZZK-help-ZZZZK-trouble!"

"Listen up, everybot!" Bumblebee says. "There seems to be a glitch. Let's pick it up and return to base."

As the Autobots charge forward, a dark figure swoops overhead. It screeches loudly as it dive-bombs toward Team Bee.

The Autobots cover their audio receptors, losing their grip on the trussed-up trouble-maker.

"SHINY!" Filch squawks, eyeing the metallic sheen of Scuzzard's body.

She digs her talons into his back, and the sharp pain jostles him into consciousness.

"AAAH!" Scuzzard cries.

Filch quickly extends her wings with expert grace and speed, lifting Scuzzard into the air and carrying him away.

The howling Scuzzard hurls insults at his attacker until both fugitives are far beyond the reach of the Autobots.

Sideswipe blinks in disbelief and turns to Strongarm.

"*Sweet solus prime!*" he exclaims. "Was that—"

"Yes," Strongarm replies.

"Did she just—"

"Yes."

"Are we in deep—"

"*Oh* yes."

Bumblebee manages to complete their sentences. "Did our *old* prisoner just fly off with our *new* prisoner?"

"YES!" Strongarm and Sideswipe yell together.

"Scrud!" Bumblebee exclaims.

The Autobots immediately shift from their robot forms into vehicle modes. They race at top speed toward the command center.

"Something must have compromised our home base," Strongarm says. "How else could Filch have escaped her stasis pod?"

"The sooner we get to the bottom of this, the sooner we can settle the score with those slag-heaps," Sideswipe adds. He revs his engine and races past Bumblebee and Strongarm, kicking up a cloud of exhaust and dust.

Bumblebee watches Sideswipe disappear down the hill before them. "Okay, Strongarm, we have to stay calm. What do you remember from our last run-in with Filch?"

"Filch is a Corvicon," Strongarm states. "She has a compulsion to hoard objects with extremely shiny and reflective surfaces. That explains her immediate seizure of Scuzzard. Last time we tussled, she was storing all her stolen goods in the headpiece of the Crown City Colossus. It is unclear where her nest will be at this juncture, or if she has acquired one yet."

"That's why we need to keep our optics wide and be ready for anything," Bumblebee replies.

Finally, the Autobots arrive at the scrapyard and change back into bot mode. Sideswipe is already assessing the devastation inside the command center.

The outer wall has been reduced to a pile of rubble thanks to when Grimlock plowed through it. A cloud of plaster dust still hangs in the air.

Fortunately, most of the computers and monitors are still up and running, but the communication devices are on the fritz.

Grimlock, Fixit, Russell, and Denny are huddled around the stasis pods. The chamber that once held Filch lies on its side, open and littered with debris.

"I'm such a klutz-o-tron!" Grimlock cries.

"Tell us what happened," Bumblebee says.

Russell recounts the events that transpired earlier, leading up to Filch's escape.

Bumblebee consoles the Dinobot.

"It's all right, Grimlock. Let's look at the fuel gauge as half full, shall we?"

He hopes that his positive attitude will be contagious.

"How can I?" Grimlock wails. "This is a massive mistake!"

Denny steps in and tries to lighten the mood. "It just so happens, Fixit has been itching to repair something all day. Maybe this is an opportunity in disguise?"

"Great to hear," Bumblebee says.

"Well, little buddies," Denny says to Fixit and Russell. "The pinball machine can wait."

With his dad, Russell grabs the downed end of the stasis pod and they tilt it back upright. Fixit reconfigures his arm into a hyper-span regulator so that he may begin repairs on the damaged chamber.

Strongarm turns to her team leader and asks, "What's *our* next course of action?"

Bumblebee crosses over to the command center's main console and pulls up the holo-scroll. "Hmm, it appears there are two active Decepticon signals in our vicinity. Must be Scuzzard and Filch."

"They haven't gotten far," Sideswipe says. "If we act fast, we may still catch up to them!"

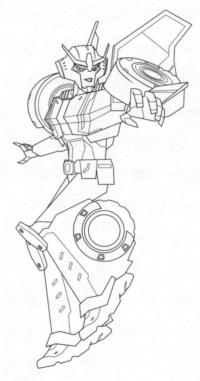

"We *have* to act fast," Strongarm adds. "Or else they'll fly back into the city and put all those civilians at risk."

"Precisely, Strongarm," Bumblebee says. "This time we'll need to combine *all* our forces to take them down."

Grimlock lifts his head with pride as the team leader looks his way.

"Here's the play, Team Bee," Bumblebee commands. "Get out there and cage those birdbots!"

Chapter 9

The sun sets over Crown City, and its citizens are unaware of two large winged creatures soaring high above the skyline.

Filch is flying toward the amusement park, attracted by its blinking lights and bright colorful surfaces. She plans to build a new nest atop the Ferris wheel.

"SHINY!" she squeals.

Scuzzard is less enthusiastic.

"Unhand me at once!" he commands.

Filch ignores her captive.

Furious, Scuzzard bites down hard on the Corvicon's foot.

Filch howls and drops the Scavengebot into the empty bumper car pavilion.

SMASH!

Looking around, Scuzzard is pleased with his new surroundings.

"This isn't exactly the central plaza at Kaon, but it definitely deserves a good thrashing," Scuzzard says. "It's hideous!"

He immediately lays waste to the bumper cars. Once they are reduced to scrap, he eats them one by one. His body shimmers and increases in size until he is as big as the pavilion itself!

The Decepticon bursts through the roof of the tent. He looms ominously over the amusement park, casting a dark shadow with his imposing form.

"I'm large and in charge!" Scuzzard cackles.

The Scavengebot sets his sights on the scrumptious skyline of Crown City in the distance.

"Now, *there's* the main course!"

Fearing that her new territory is being threatened, Filch dive-bombs toward Scuzzard. She head butts him in the chest, knocking him off balance.

BAM!

The gigantic robot lurches backward over

the pavilion and crash-lands in the parking lot of Doug's Den.

Seconds later, Scuzzard rises back to his full height. Filch torpedoes toward him once again. The massive monster plucks his flying foe out of the air and crunches her in his grip.

"You won't catch *me* off guard this time, but I'll catch *you*!" he jeers.

At that very moment, Bumblebee and his team of Autobots speed into the parking lot. Grimlock looks up in awe.

"Whoa! Scavengebot versus Corvicon? This is better than Rumbledome!" he shouts.

Scuzzard turns his attention toward the new arrivals and smiles wickedly. "The fun has just begun! Let's play whack-a-bot!"

He stomps and pounds the pavement with

his enormous feet as the heroes scramble to evade being crushed. They swerve and dodge the rapid assault from above, narrowly missing one another.

"Ha! Now I'll get to see some Autobot bumper cars in action!" Scuzzard says with a laugh.

"Your wish is our command sequence!" Sideswipe cries, burning rubber.

He slams right into the Decepticon's foot.

BAM!

"Way to take the lead, Sideswipe," Bumblebee says.

Bumblebee and Strongarm follow their friend and bash into the humongous Decepticon's other foot.

They drive in reverse and then slam into his feet again as if they really are bumper cars!

"Enough games," Scuzzard bellows. "You are nothing but nanodrones to me!"

He hurls Filch at the Autobots, and she lands on top of Bumblebee. The yellow sports car and the Corvicon speed across the parking lot until they come to a screeching halt. Neither of them moves.

Strongarm races to her lieutenant's side.

"Keep that Scavengebot occupied until we can regroup!" she calls out to Sideswipe and Grimlock.

"Hey, birdbrain!" Grimlock shouts at Scuzzard. "I've taken down bigger bots than you with my Dino-Destructo Double Drop!"

"I'd be shocked if that were true," Scuzzard replies. "But I'm willing to let you try. Dinobots make me laugh!"

The Decepticon advances on Grimlock and kneels down to face him.

Sideswipe uses this opportunity to change into his bot mode and springs into action. He sprints toward a nearby lamppost, swings around it with the agility of an acrobat, and leaps onto an adjacent telephone pole. Then he hurls himself off the top and lands right on Scuzzard's back.

"Let's get ready to Rumbledome!" Sideswipe yells.

The flashy Autobot punches the Decepticon right in the head.

POW!

Grimlock follows suit and jumps onto Scuzzard, too.

ROARRR!

"You've got double trouble now!" he quips, and bashes the big robot with his tail.

In the meantime, Strongarm changes into her robot form upon reaching Bumblebee. She pushes Filch off the team leader. The Decepticon twitches and starts to stir.

Bumblebee revives first and quickly shifts into bot mode.

"We have to stop Scuzzard!" he exclaims.

Strongarm guides his gaze to the gargantuan villain and says, "He's got a lot on his mind right now, sir."

Bumblebee beams with pride watching his teammates work together.

Suddenly, a screeching voice pierces their audio receptors.

"SHINY!"

Filch is on her feet and ready to attack.

Bumblebee and Strongarm deploy their neo-forges again and will them to take the shape of an energy staff and crossbow.

Filch charges Bumblebee, pecking at him

with her beak. The Autobot parries with the staff and directs an energy blast at his flying foe.

ZAP!

The Decepticon falls to the ground.

Strongarm shoots an energized grappling hook from her crossbow that loops around Filch's body. The Corvicon hisses and bucks as the glowing rope ties tight.

"We got us a live one here, sir!" Strongarm grunts.

On the other side of the arcade's parking lot, Sideswipe and Grimlock continue to tag-team Scuzzard.

Grimlock throws a jab.

WHACK!

Sideswipe follows with a right hook.

WHAP!

Grimlock lands an uppercut.

WHAM!

Disoriented, the Decepticon flails his arms. One of them catches Grimlock and swats the Dinobot onto the pavement.

THUD!

Scuzzard lifts his leg and prepares to make street pizza out of Grimlock.

Sideswipe acts fast and covers the Scavengebot's optics with his hands. Scuzzard whirls around blindly while the Autobot guides him toward a telephone pole.

Scuzzard stumbles and his upper body gets tangled in the power lines. Sideswipe swiftly slides down the pole to safety as volts of electricity surge through the wires and over-load the Decepticon in a shower of sparks!

ZAAAAAAAARK!

Scuzzard spasms and jolts as he shrinks back to his normal size. Finally, he slumps headfirst into a crumpled, smoldering heap.

BOOM!

"Aw, yeah!" Sideswipe cheers. "Team Bee always brings the buzz!"

Grimlock laughs. "Yeah, he looks a little *shocked*!"

All of a sudden, more electricity crackles behind the duo. They turn to see an illumi-nated portal light up the night sky.

It is an activated Groundbridge and out from it emerges the bounty hunter and their teammate Drift. "I believe I can be of some assistance," he says.

"Nah, we got everything under control," replies Sideswipe.

Suddenly, someone screams.

"AAAAAAAAH!"

Sideswipe, Grimlock, and Drift turn to see Strongarm hoisted off the ground. She is clutching her crossbow, which is attached to Filch, who is soaring high into the air!

The Corvicon flaps her wings faster and faster, dragging the Autobot along for a wild ride.

Pulling Scuzzard with them, the other three Autobots rush over to their leader.

"What's the plan, Bee?" Sideswipe cries.

"Gridlock Grimlock!" Bumblebee exclaims.

"Reporting for duty," the Dinobot calls out.

"Strongarm is going long, and I need you to make the pass," says Bumblebee.

"With what?" Grimlock asks.

"Me."

The plan dawns on the Dinobot and he picks up their leader.

Grimlock winds up and snaps Bumblebee into the air. Bumblebee slices through the night sky like a rocket and reaches Strongarm in seconds.

Bumblebee grips her feet, and their combined weight slows Filch down. The trio begins a descent toward the asphalt below.

At that very moment, Doug comes out of the arcade to investigate the commotion behind his store—and is immediately dumbstruck!

He sees Drift and Sideswipe standing over Scuzzard, and Grimlock watching Bumblebee and Strongarm touch down with Filch in tow.

"Scrap!" Sideswipe shouts when he sees the man. "Let's make tracks!"

The young Autobot and the bounty hunter drag Scuzzard into the Groundbridge.

Grimlock helps Bumblebee and Strongarm yank Filch into the portal also before it closes behind them in a blinding flash.

Doug takes off his glasses, rubs his eyes, and puts the glasses back on. He searches the empty parking lot, but the sentient robots have disappeared.

"I must be playing too many video games," he says.

Chapter 10

Team Bee appears at the scrapyard in an instant. The Autobots find themselves behind the tall tower of cars where Grimlock was napping earlier that morning.

Fixit contacts them from the command center.

"Is everybot in one piece?" he asks.

Before they can answer, Filch sees the cars and screeches.

"MORE SHINY!" she squawks.

In a flash, she expands her wings, shoving Bumblebee and Strongarm to the ground. The other Autobots give chase, but the Corvicon is too fast.

Filch flies up to the top of the tower and heaves it with all her might. Tipping and toppling, the cars come crashing down in an avalanche of heavy metal.

"Brace yourselves!" Drift shouts.

With lightning speed, the bounty hunter unsheathes his energy sword and cleaves the first falling car in half. Then he nimbly somersaults out of harm's way.

Bumblebee and the others fire their blasters

at the vehicles, but the onslaught overpowers them.

CHOOM!

CHOOM!

SLAM!

Drift watches in horror as his comrades-in-arms get buried under a pile of used cars. Then he sees Filch heading toward the command center. He is faced with a decision: save his teammates or stop the Decepticon?

Bumblebee emits a muffled cry.

"Drift...help..."

"Jetstorm, Slipstream," he calls out. "Heed your master!"

Jetstorm and Slipstream are Drift's mini-con apprentices who reside upon his armor.

At his command, they hop off and spring into action.

"The captive Corvicon has escaped... again!" announces Drift. "But I must assist my fellow soldiers."

"Of course, master. We're off!"

Jetstorm and Slipstream bow and then zip after Filch. Fixit uploads coordinates directly into their mainframes, instructing them where to guide the Corvicon.

As the mini-cons zigzag through the scrapyard, they scrape their limbs across the metal nearby. The screeching sound and shower of sparks catch Filch's attention.

She hones in on the mini-cons and squeals.

"SHINY! For my collection!"

Jetstorm and Slipstream bank left down a crowded aisle. Filch dives after them and chases the mini-cons until they come to a clearing.

And at the end of the aisle, Denny, Russell, and Fixit are waiting for them. They are driving the hydraulic truck!

The two mini-cons split up and zoom in opposite directions, confusing the speeding Corvicon. She flaps her wings to slow down, but it is too late.

Denny activates the magnet and extracts Filch from her flight path straight above!

CLANG!

The Decepticon dangles helplessly while screeching in distress.

"Looks like we're adding you back into *our* collection," Russell replies.

Moments later, the Autobots reconvene at

the command center. They look a little worse for wear but are relieved that the Decepticon disaster was finally brought to an end.

Together, they deposit Scuzzard and Filch back into the repaired stasis pods.

"Who says there's no excitement at the scrapyard?" Sideswipe says with a smile.

Russell smiles back and replies, "To be honest, I wouldn't mind some quiet time around here."

"We can always play pinball!" Denny adds with a laugh.

As the group finds itself in a harmonious mood, Bumblebee turns to Drift and says, "Thank you for your assistance today."

"Think nothing of it," Drift says. "It takes a strong Autobot and great leader to ask for help."

"Agreed," Bumblebee nods. He looks at Strongarm, Sideswipe, Fixit, and Grimlock. "There is no problem too big that can't be handled with teamwork," he says.

"And that includes a three-story Decepticon!" Sideswipe adds.

"We accomplished our mission and became better teammates thanks to you, sir," Strongarm says to Bumblebee. "I'm positive Optimus Prime would be very proud."

"Speaking of phenomenal forces," Drift interrupts. "There is indeed a batch of Energon in a quadrant not too far from here. We can set our course for the power source in the morning."

"Awesome," Bumblebee says. "It will definitely give us an advantage in future battles against the Decepticons."

"I agree with you, boss," Grimlock tells his leader. "But don't you think we all deserve to recharge a bit? I know *I* do."

And with that, the Dinobot curls up outside the command center and falls fast asleep.

Drift's Samurai Showdown

TRANSFORMERS
ROBOTS IN DISGUISE

Drift's Samurai Showdown

by John Sazaklis & Steve Foxe

"Decepticon attack!" Bumblebee shouts at his team. "The scrapyard has been breached!" He zooms through their makeshift Earth headquarters with his high-beam lights flashing and his horn blaring. "All bots to their stations! This is *not* a drill!"

Strongarm is the first Autobot to respond to Bee's alerts, switching straight from sleep mode to her robot form. This eager cadet is always at the ready.

"I'll protect the humans, sir!" she says, sprinting toward the vintage diner that Denny and Russell Clay call home. "I can see Sideswipe isn't up to the task!"

"Hey, this bot's always got his motor revving," replies Sideswipe, flexing his gears and

shaking out his sprockets. "It just so happens to be the middle of a night cycle, and I was getting my beauty recharge."

The flashy, young Sideswipe flips through the air and lands back-to-back against the straightlaced Strongarm.

Suddenly, the ground beneath them starts to rumble at the approach of pounding footsteps. The two Autobots draw their weapons.

"AWW YEAH, LET ME AT 'EM!" Grimlock roars, stomping his way toward the scrapyard's front gate.

The massive Dinobot is *always* itching to turn some Decepticons into scrap metal!

Bumblebee screeches to a halt in Grimlock's path, blocking his stampede.

"That's not the plan, Grim. Follow our breach protocol!"

Bumblebee spins his wheels while the Dinobot complies and turns around. Grimlock joins his teammates at the diner, grumbling all the way.

Denny Clay stumbles out into the scrapyard he owns and operates, rubbing the sleep from his eyes and tying the belt on his vintage rockabilly flamingo robe a little tighter.

"What's all this racket? It's after midnight, you know," Denny pleads, stifling a yawn. "Humans actually *need* to sleep, remember?"

Bumblebee pulls up next to the diner and shifts into bot mode. With his lights still shining, the Autobot leader peers into the darkness of the scrapyard. There are no

Decepticons in sight. There's also no sign of Drift, the stoic and mysterious former bounty hunter who recently joined up with them.

"Where's Drift?" Bumblebee asks. "This breach-defense drill needs full cooperation to work."

Strongarm and Sideswipe exchange looks as they slowly realize the "Decepticon attack"

may not be as real as they had thought. They return their weapons to their holsters.

"Um, sir, did you say 'drill'?" Strongarm asks tentatively.

If any bot understands the need for preparedness, it's Strongarm, but that doesn't mean she appreciates being left in the dark by her commanding officer.

Russell Clay, Denny's twelve-year-old son, steps out from behind a row of antique washing machines. He clicks a stopwatch in his hand.

"Three minutes and forty-five seconds, Bee," Russell says. "Two minutes longer than your goal time."

"Scrap, that's no good. And Drift didn't even show up! I don't know about that bot...." Bumblebee sighs. "In the case of a Decepticon attack on the scrapyard during typical Earth rest hours, we should all be able to meet at Central Diner Defense Point Delta in under two minutes."

Grimlock is still ready to rumble. He looks around and slowly—more slowly than the other bots—realizes what's going on.

"Wait a nanocycle...you mean I don't get to demolish any Decepticons tonight?"

"No, Grim," Bumblebee explains. "This was meant to be a team-training exercise, but not all your teammates thought it was worth their time."

As the Autobots begin to disperse, Drift calmly joins the gathering, flanked by his two Mini-Cons, Jetstorm and Slipstream.

"Nice of you to show up," Sideswipe mumbles.

"It is wise of you to train your team, Bumblebee," Drift says dryly. "It is clear that they struggle with basic functions."

Drift's deadpan insult noticeably upsets Strongarm, who prides herself on her professionalism and combat readiness. "But I do not need training. I have survived on my own for many cycles," he continues.

Jetstorm coughs as if to remind Drift that he has been alone *except* for his Mini-Cons. Slipstream steps on Jetstorm's foot and quiets the less reserved of the two apprentice-bots. Drift is a stern master and doesn't appreciate his students speaking out of turn.

"I know you're used to working alone, Drift," Bumblebee says, taking on an air of authority. "And I'm happy to have you as part of our team here on Earth. But I won't stand for you insulti—"

BREEP! BREEP!

An alarm screeches over the speaker system installed on the diner's exterior.

"Decepticon attack! Please retort...resort... report to the command center at once!" The jumble of words is the telltale malfunction of Fixit, the Autobots' Mini-Con helper.

Denny Clay covers his ears with his hands.

"Is this another drill, Bee?" Denny yells over the siren. "If so, it's way past Rusty's bedtime—and mine!"

"If this is a drill, it's not one I planned!" Bumblebee yells back. "We better join Fixit and find out what's going on!"

Once everyone gathers in the command center, Fixit taps furiously at his console to pull up a large hologram of the Decepticon his systems discovered. The villainous bot is short and round, with a masklike marking over his eyes and a large tail circled by rings of alternating black and brown metal.

"Aw yeah, I get to smash up a Decepticon!" Grimlock says, pounding his fists together.

"Hey, he looks like a raccoon!" Russell observes.

"What's a 'raccoon'?" Grimlock asks. "That's not like a"— he gulps —"kitten, is it?"

The typically bombastic Dinobot looks oddly nervous. He's not very good at hiding his bizarre fear of Earth felines.

"Actually, they're not closely related,"

Russell says, easing Grimlock's mind slightly. "But they do look and act a little similar, I guess."

Grimlock suppresses a startled yelp.

"My sensors picked up a Decepticon moving through the side streets of Crown City," Fixit explains. "It appears that he is trying to stay hidden from humans, but who knows how long that will last!"

"All right, bots, we need to apprehend this Decepticon before he's spotted," Bee says, stepping up to lead his team.

"Oh, he's not spotted," Sideswipe remarks, pointing at the image. "He's striped, see?"

Bumblebee narrows his optics.

"What?" Sideswipe shrugs. "I may be

half-charged, but my funny bolt is always at one hundred percent!"

Ignoring the hotshot Autobot, Bumblebee continues with the task at hand.

"Grim, you'll have to stay behind. We'll be in the middle of the city, and you don't have a vehicle mode," he says.

The Dinobot tries to hide his relief.

"Fixit, what can you tell us about this criminal before we put wheels down and go to town?" Bumblebee asks.

Sideswipe groans over Bee's attempt at a catchphrase.

"Decepticon identification: Forager. Mercenary, bounty hunter, and rabble-rouser," Fixit says as he punches at the console processing data. "Arrested alongside other Decepticons calling themselves the Ronin."

Drift scoffs. "This Decepticon is not worth my time. I will provide you with my students, Jetstorm and Sliptstream, to assist in my absence."

Before Bumblebee can protest, Drift turns and walks out of the room.

"I guess someone never learned teamwork in lob-ball youth league," Sideswipe whispers loudly to Rusty.

"Okay, team, we don't have time for this. We've got to put wheels down and—"

"Bee!" the rest of the room shouts in unison, cutting off their leader's mediocre new rallying cry.

"Fine, let's just go capture this Decepticon," Bumblebee says, leaping into vehicle mode and leading his team out of the scrapyard.

Slipstream and Jetstorm jump onto Sideswipe's trailer and Strongarm brings up the rear. Grimlock and Fixit stay behind as the yawning pair of Clays shuffle off to bed.

The Autobots cut through the forest, cross the bridge, and arrive in Crown City in no time. Using Fixit's coordinates, they quickly spot Forager in a dark alley behind an auto repair store.

The dexterous Decepticon is sifting through spare parts.

Bumblebee quietly directs Sideswipe to

take to the rooftops. The younger bot zooms out of view, switches back to bot mode, and leaps into the air with Slipstream and Jetstorm in tow.

Strongarm, in her police SUV mode, pulls around to block Forager's exit.

Once the whole team is in place, Bee honks his horn—*BEEP BEEP*—startling the Decepticon!

"Oh, scrud, guess I gotta bust up some natives!" Forager growls, tearing an old tire in two with his bare paws. "Let's dance!"

"Heads up!" Sideswipe yells, drawing his swords and dropping down from above.

The two Mini-Cons follow close behind.

Sideswipe slashes and slices at Forager with his blades.

SWISH!

CLANG!

The Decepticon deflects the blows with his claws as showers of sparks light up the night sky.

Slipstream and Jetstorm lunge at Forager's legs.

The cranky crook hops from one foot to the other, trying to kick the Mini-Cons off.

"Looks like we are dancing after all!" says Jetstorm.

While Forager attempts to hold off his three ninja-like assailants, Strongarm and Bumblebee rev their engines and charge at the Decepticon.

In a flash, the two Autobots crunch Forager between their fenders!

SMASH!

The craven convict is down for the count.

"Good work, team," Bumblebee says.

The Autobots load Forager's unconscious frame onto the trailer, tie him down, and cover him with a tarp.

Bumblebee radios Fixit and asks the Mini-Con to prepare a stasis pod.

A short victory lap later, the bots arrive back at the scrapyard with their defeated target.

"My, that was fast!" Fixit exclaims, greeting the bots near the stasis pods. "Not much fight in this one?"

"This is just what happens when you work together, Fixit," Bumblebee says, scanning the scrapyard for Drift. "Too bad not everyone on this team seems to have gotten the memo."

As if on cue, Drift rounds the corner.

Slipstream and Jetstorm bow to their master.

"I am glad the mission went well," Drift says. "I trust my students were of sufficient help?"

Slipstream bows and pulls back the tarp to reveal a still-unconscious Forager. Drift gives a barely perceptible nod of approval.

Once the Mini-Con replaces the cover, Forager opens his optics. The raccoon-like bot was playing possum! He flexes his dexterous paws, and two lockpicks pop out from the tips of his claws. With a swift twist of his wrist, Forager frees himself and makes a break for it, tossing the tarp at Drift and the Mini-Cons to distract them!

"So long, losers—"

WHAM!

Forager runs smack-dab into Grimlock.

"Looks like I got to demolish a Decepticon after all!" Grim says, proudly holding Forager down with one massive foot.

Bumblebee helps Grim load the struggling captive into the designated stasis pod.

"Let go of me! I have rights, you know!"

Forager yells, straining against Grimlock's powerful grip. "You can't lock me up just 'cause I'm a convicted criminal!"

Before the pod's cover slides shut, Forager gets a good look at the other bots. His optics lock on Drift.

"Hey! I know you!" Forager hollers, pointing at Drift through the stasis pod window. "From that Ronin job on the moon of Athena! You gotta get me outta here, pal!"

Before Forager can say anything else, Fixit finishes the stasis sequence and puts the dangerous Decepticon on ice.

Bumblebee quietly mouths Forager's words to himself, processing what was just said. He turns toward Drift.

"What did he mean by 'pal'?"

Drift tenses his shoulders. The mysterious samurai rests one hand on the hilt of his sword.

"My past is my own, Bumblebee. Do not assume you have any right to know about it."

Strongarm and Sideswipe move closer to Bumblebee's side.

"If you're going to work alongside my team, I think I have every right."

Jetstorm and Slipstream cast worried glances at their master, who refuses to meet their optics.

"If that is your stance, perhaps it is time I leave this team, Bumblebee." Drift quickly shifts into his vehicle mode and speeds out of the scrapyard!

As the dust settles, everyone exchanges grave looks.

Everyone except for Grimlock.

"So, uh, what just happened?"

Chapter 3

Denny Clay's alarm clock goes off at seven
o'clock the next morning. Crawling out of
bed to the sound of golden oldies, Denny's
first thought is that the Autobots can keep
their Energon—he just wants his coffee!

The Clays enjoy having Bee and the others around, but it can make for a lot of sleepless nights, something that exhausts Denny a bit more than it does his preteen son, Russell.

As the man shuffles outside half-awake, he stumbles upon a full-on Autobot interrogation, like something out of one of his favorite vintage cops-versus-gangsters films.

Slipstream and Jetstorm are sitting side-by-side on an overturned refrigerator. Bumblebee leans over the tiny bots, scowling, while Grimlock, Strongarm, and Sideswipe stand menacingly behind him.

"Youse better fess up, or it's no more Mr. Nice-Bot!" Bumblebee says, affecting a bizarre accent.

"Whoa, guys, what's going on here?" Denny asks, sprinting toward them as fast as his retro bunny slippers will carry him. "And what's with that corny gangster act, Bee?"

"Sometimes you leave the TV on at night, and that stuff starts to sink in," Bumblebee replies. "Besides, we tried asking nicely, but these two won't say a word."

"Why are you questioning your own guys?"

Denny asks, surprised at Bumblebee's behavior. "And where's Drift? I don't think he'd like you going off on his students like this."

"That's exactly the problem, sir," Strongarm pipes in. "Our newest Decepticon prisoner seemed to recognize Drift as a former ally, but Drift sped away before we could get any explanation out of him. Now we're questioning his Mini-Cons to try to uncover if Drift is actually an embedded Decepticon agent!"

Bumblebee steps forward to apologize to the frightened Slipstream and Jetstorm. Being a leader isn't easy. Even Optimus occasionally made the wrong call.

"I'm sorry. We might have...overreacted," Bumblebee says. "We're happy to have Drift and the two of you on the team, and it's admirable that you want to protect him, but we really need to know what's going on."

Slipstream and Jetstorm look at each other, their optics widening and narrowing in wordless conversation. Jetstorm opens his mouth to speak, but Slipstream glares at him to stay quiet.

Soon, Russell Clay wanders outside, sleepy-eyed and confused.

"What's going on out here, Bee?" Russell asks.

After Bee fills Russell in on the Mini-Cons' strict silence, Russell steps forward to take charge.

"Why don't you let me have a shot with

them?" Russell asks, cracking his knuckles. Slipstream and Jetstorm would have been intimidated, but it's hard to be scared of an Earth boy in cartoon-print pajamas. "Give me a few minutes and I'll have them singing like stool pigeons."

"I don't need them to sing; I just need them to talk," Bumblebee says, prompting an exaggerated eye roll from Russell.

"I know I can do it," Russell says with confidence. "But you'd better give us some space. Except for you, Sideswipe. You should stay."

Everyone else reluctantly heads to the opposite end of the scrapyard. Denny shoots Russell a look of concern before he goes, but Russell gives his dad a thumbs-up. Once the others are out of sight, Russell climbs onto Sideswipe's shoulders.

"Okay, boys, it's time to play rough," he says, looming over the Mini-Cons. "Tag, you're it!"

Russell leans down and slaps Jetstorm on the shoulder, then shouts at Sideswipe to run. After a moment's confusion, Sideswipe grins and runs off through one of the winding corridors of junk and old trash that makes up the scrapyard.

Jetstorm and Slipstream share a puzzled glance before Jetstorm cracks a sly grin, too, and runs off after Sideswipe. With a drawn-out sigh, Slipstream follows.

"Tag, you're it!" Jetstorm shrieks, knocking Sideswipe on the knee.

"Not for long!" Sideswipe replies, leaping backward to bop an unamused Slipstream on the head. "Tag! Your turn!"

Slipstream grumbles and refuses to move, but he can't deny wanting to play, too. He runs after his fellow Mini-Con and tags him, keeping the game in motion until Russell is a sweaty mess and the three bots are running on fumes.

They all meet back by the diner and plop down near the overturned fridge.

"So, how does that count as interrogation, Russell Clay?" Jetstorm asks, stretching out his joints.

"It doesn't. I figured you get enough of that just by being Drift's students," Russell replies. "He's really tough on you two."

Slipstream and Jetstorm look at each other and slowly nod.

"Master Drift *is* tough on us, but it's for our own good," Slipstream says, defending their master. "And whatever he's doing now, whatever reason he has for leaving, must be a good one."

"So you don't know why that Decepticon might act like he knew Drift?" Russell asks.

"Master Drift shares lessons with us, not his life story," Slipstream replies.

Jetstorm coughs and nudges Slipstream in the side. Slipstream tries to act like he doesn't notice, but Jetstorm does it again—and again. Finally, Slipstream comes out with it.

"Okay, fine!" Slipstream whispers angrily. "Master Drift did tell us one thing that is probably important...."

Russell and Sideswipe lean in to hear Slipstream's hushed information.

"Before Master Drift was Master Drift," explains Slipstream, "he went by another name: Deadlock. And under that name, Master Drift wasn't the honorable Autobot hero you know today—he was a Decepticon!"

Chapter 4

"Drift used to be a Decepticon?! Are you serious?" Bumblebee shouts, leaping out from behind a pile of old bicycles. "We let a traitor into our ranks?"

Strongarm climbs out from her own hiding spot under a stack of vintage carousel horses.

"You couldn't have known, sir!" she says.

"Decepticons are deceptive—why, it's right there in the name! Although, there is protocol in place for background checks. If you had read handbook entry eight hundred sixteen, subsection eighty-seven, you'd know that...."

"Not helpful, Strongarm!" Russell says. "And were you guys spying on us? Didn't you trust us?!"

"Yeah, didn't you trust them, Bee?" Grimlock asks, peering down from the roof of a nearby retired school bus. Russell shoots him an accusing look. "Hey, don't look at me. I just come up here to catch some sun once in a while." The Dinobot lies back down on his perch and stretches out, excusing himself from the conversation.

Bumblebee stands up to address Russell and the Mini-Cons.

"I do trust you, Russell, and I appreciate the honesty, Slipstream and Jetstorm," he says. "But this is very serious. If Drift was communicating with Forager, he might also have been communicating with Steeljaw or other, even worse Decepticons. He could have been getting close to us to feed them intel on how to attack Earth."

"Master Drift would never betray his word!" Slipstream shouts. "Master Drift is a bot of honor. He would never betray...us."

Slipstream hangs his head in disappointment. Jetstorm moves to comfort his brother-in-arms, but Slipstream pulls away.

Sideswipe mulls over everything he's heard

from Slipstream and Bumblebee, along with the scene he witnessed last night. The typically hasty bot tries to recall exactly what Forager said to Drift before the stasis pod closed.

"Hey, Bee, I just thought of something," Sideswipe says. "Forager said he recognized Drift from a moon or something, but it wasn't an instant thing, right? He had to think about it first."

Slipstream and Jetstorm look up at Sideswipe hopefully.

"So maybe Drift does have, you know, a past—just like Grim—but it's all behind him now, and he's just ashamed to admit it? We've all done things we aren't proud of."

Bumblebee considers this thoughtfully.

Grimlock leans back over the roof of the bus to nod encouragingly.

"Well, sir, Sideswipe may be right," Strongarm says, "but we have to consider the possibility that Drift is no longer allied with Forager and is afraid of compromising plans with other Decepticons."

Slipstream and Jetstorm both groan in frustration.

"I'm sorry, sir, but we can't afford to take chances," Strongarm adds. "We've already witnessed infighting among the Decepticons, so we need to be prepared for any outcome."

"I'm afraid Strongarm is right," Bumblebee says, addressing the Mini-Cons. "It might be hard to hear, but we have to brace ourselves for the worst until we can find Drift and get his side of this. And it doesn't make me optimistic that he sped off when we tried to discuss it."

The Autobots and Russell slowly trudge back toward the diner, their minds swirling with thoughts of betrayal and mistrust.

Suddenly, Fixit's voice crackles over the speaker system.

"This is not a drill! Multiple Decepticon signals located!"

The Autobots all rush to the command

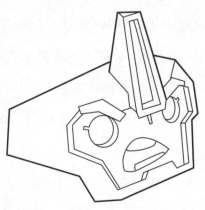

center, where Fixit pulls up a holographic map. Two red beacons flash in the quarry a few miles from the scrapyard.

"Fixit, can you pull up information on these new Decepticons so we know who we're facing?" Bee asks.

Fixit's digits click-clack across the keyboard. He buzzes with confusion.

"I'm afraid not, Bee," Fixit replies. "It looks like these Decepticons have obscured their signals!"

"Can you look up another signal for us?" Strongarm asks. "Can you track Drift?"

The Mini-Con goes back to speedily typing away. After a moment, Fixit shouts, "Aha!" and turns back around.

"Our systems are too weak to pick up most general bot signals unless they're in the immediate area, but by rerouting the signal booster through the Energon relay—"

"Cut to the chase, please, Fixit," Bumblebee interrupts politely.

"Base...case...I mean, 'chase' indeed, Bee!" Fixit replies, pointing to the screen. "There's a signal that matches Drift's size and shape moving right toward the two Decepticons!"

Slipstream and Jetstorm give each other worried looks—as do Bee and Strongarm, but for different reasons.

"We must find and assist Master Drift!" Jetstorm pleads. "We don't know how powerful those Decepticons might be, and he's headed right for them!"

Bumblebee agrees with the Mini-Con. He orders everyone to gather up and head out, except for Jetstorm and Slipstream. The disappointment is clear on their faces.

"You two stay behind and protect Russell, Denny, and Fixit in case one of the Decepticons breaks away and comes here," Bee instructs. "We'll go help your master."

The two smaller bots reluctantly accept the Autobot leader's commands. Bee changes into his shiny yellow vehicle mode and leads Strongarm, Sideswipe, and Grimlock out the gate, racing into the woods toward the three signals.

Once they're out of earshot of the others, Strongarm drives up close to Bee and whispers to her commanding officer.

"Sir, you know there's a possibility that Drift is moving toward the Decepticons *on purpose*, right?" Strongarm says. She hesitates, not wanting to finish saying what she's thinking. "That he might be meeting up with his—"

"Don't say it, Strongarm," Bee interrupts. "I know what you're thinking. And I'm afraid your suspicion might be right. Drift isn't accidentally heading toward trouble—he's meeting up with his Decepticon allies to cause it!"

As Bumblebee, Strongarm, Sideswipe, and Grimlock race toward the Decepticon beacons, Russell does his best to keep Drift's anxious Mini-Cons occupied at the scrapyard.

"Tag, you're it!" Russell shouts, bopping Jetstorm on the shoulder and running off. The Mini-Con does not move to follow.

"I am not it, Russell Clay," Jetstorm replies morosely. "Unless 'it' means 'depressed.'"

Russell frowns. He turns to his dad for help.

"Hey, guys!" Denny says in his characteristically cheery voice. "I just got a shipment of retro video-game cartridges, and I need help blowing on them to see which ones still work. Think you guys are fit for duty?"

Jetstorm and Slipstream are too honorbound to resist a call to help. They both stand at once and bow to Denny.

"We will assist you in your task, Denny Clay," they say in unison.

"Yeah, that sounds great!" Fixit adds. "Maybe while we do that, I can tell you all about how I once subdivided the power coupler to—"

"Sure thing, Fixit," Denny says, cutting him off. "Whatever floats your boat."

"Oh, Denny Clay," Fixit chuckles. "This was on a trans-galactic space shuttle, not a boat! Really, humans are so odd sometimes."

As the Clays keep the Mini-Cons occupied, the Autobots zoom through the woods toward the flashing beacons. Bee screeches to a stop at the edge of the forest where the trees clear and the land slopes down into the quarry.

"Okay, bots, this is where Fixit's tracker

leads," Bumblebee whispers, changing into robot mode and peering down at the device in his hands. "That means Drift should be right…there!"

Bumblebee points across the quarry, where Drift's sleek sports car form kicks up a storm of dust. "But where are the Decepticons? The tracker shows that Drift is nearly on top of them."

"Maybe they're camouflaged!" suggests Strongarm.

"Maybe they're really small!" offers Sideswipe.

"Maybe they're ghosts!" adds Grimlock, prompting blank looks from his teammates. "What? Rusty always makes me watch scary movies with him. You never know!"

Bumblebee quiets his team. As they watch, Drift rushes right past the Decepticon signals and plows into the forest on the other side of the quarry.

"There's something strange going on here," Bumblebee says, leaping into vehicle mode once more. "Follow me."

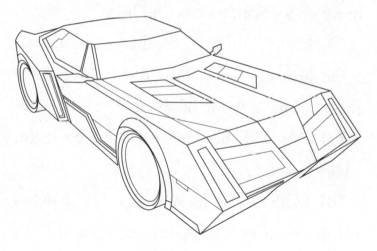

The Autobot leader steers down into the quarry, taking the same path Drift just blazed. The dust is still settling when they arrive at the location of the beacons. Bumblebee, Strongarm, and Sideswipe switch back to their bot modes.

"Great, so Fixit created another busted invention," Sideswipe says, looking around the seemingly empty quarry. "Can we get a move on and catch up with Drift?"

"Wait a minute, exhaust-for-brains," Strongarm says, crouching down. "What are these?" The law-bot holds up a pair of small metal discs with blinking red lights on them. "They look like—"

"BOMBS!" Grimlock shouts. He snatches the discs out of Strongarm's hands and hurls them across the quarry. "EVERYONE, DOWN!" The Dinobot hits the ground with a thud and the other bots follow. After a minute with no explosion, Sideswipe raises his head.

"Uhh, guys, shouldn't we have blown up by now?" the young Autobot says, peering around.

"Be quiet, Sideswipe!" Strongarm hisses.

"Explosive ordinance protocol clearly states that—"

"Hold that thought, cadet," Bumblebee

says, springing up and running in the direction of the discs. Bumblebee picks one up, checks the tracker in his hand, and then hurls the disc back in the direction of the other Autobots, scattering them. "I knew it!"

Strongarm carefully peers out from behind a boulder. "Knew what, sir?"

"These aren't bombs. They're fake Decepticon signals," Bumblebee says, picking up the remaining disc and crushing it between his digits. "Someone left them here to distract us and get us away from the scrapyard." Bumblebee quickly dials Fixit on his communicator, but the quirky little Mini-Con doesn't pick up. "Forget Drift, we need to get back now!"

Unbeknownst to Team Bee, another set of bots is on their way toward the scrapyard. Just inside the tree line that surrounds the yard's outer fence, two escaped prisoners conspire and plot.

They are the dangerous Decepticons known as Foxtrot and Stilts. Foxtrot is a cunning and sly rust-colored bot, with a big round tail and pointed, alert audio sensors. Stilts is

all length: long legs, long neck, long beak—
with a gleaming white sheen and a bright red
crown that glints in the sun.

Both bots are safely under the cover of the
signal disruption field built into Stilts's large
wings.

"It looks like those disgusting do-gooder
Autobots just found my signal decoys," Foxtrot hisses, tapping at a console embedded in
his tail. "The microcameras captured two of
them. I'll program holo-cloaks of each, and
we can waltz into their compound with ease.
My scans show that there are just three Mini-
Cons left inside."

Foxtrot punches in a few more codes and
two small discs pop out of his tail. "Here,

you take the big green one, and I'll keep the nerdy-looking yellow one."

The Decepticons fix the discs to their chests, press a button, and, in a flash, they're covered in pitch-perfect holograms of Grimlock and Bumblebee!

"A Dinobot?" Stilts says, looking down at himself with a wicked laugh. "Guess I'll have to act extra dumb to match my new look."

Inside the diner, Fixit gets a ping that the perimeter sensors have been tripped. He pulls up a visual of "Grimlock" and "Bumblebee" walking toward the scrapyard's entrance, limping and looking wounded. Denny tells

Russell to stay put and tasks Jetstorm to watch him.

Denny, Fixit, and Slipstream sprint out to attend to the disguised Decepticons at the front gate.

"Bee, are you okay?" Denny asks. "What happened to Sideswipe and Strongarm?"

"And Master Drift!" Slipstream adds.

The bot they believe to be Grimlock cracks an awful smile full of sharp teeth. He unhooks a capsule from his waist and tosses it at Slipstream and Denny.

WHOOSH!

It explodes into a giant net on impact, trapping the two of them tightly inside!

"Nothing...yet," Stilts sneers.

He drops the hologram, revealing himself as a tall birdlike Decepticon.

Fixit tries to zoom away, but pretend-Bumblebee snatches him up.

"Not so fast, scrap metal," Foxtrot says, dropping his hologram.

He dangles the Mini-Con upside down.

"You're going to show us where you're keeping Forager. The Ronin may not follow any masters, but we take care of our own!"

Chapter 6

"Did you hear something?" Russell asks, nervously peering out the diner windows. Jetstorm gently pulls the young human back.

"Let me take a look first, Russell Clay," Jetstorm says, steeling himself for action. "I am honor-bound to protect you under your master's orders."

Russell rolls his eyes. "He's not my master, Jetstorm. He's my dad!"

Jetstorm slinks silently out the diner door. He quickly freezes in his tracks when he sees Stilts approach with Denny and Slipstream strung over his shoulder in a net! Jetstorm darts inside and pulls Russell into a back room. The front door creaks slightly as it closes.

"What was that?" Stilts asks, bending his long crane-like neck toward the sound. "I thought there were only three Mini-Cons left on this base."

Denny twists around in the net.

"I, uh, dropped my hubcap," he says.

Stilts peers over his shoulder at his captives.

"You're an odd-looking bot," the Decepticon

observes. "A little...soft to be a Cybertro-nian."

"Beep boop bop?" Denny replies.

He wiggles in the bag, doing his best impression of a robotic dance that was popular in his youth. It is not very convincing.

Stilts glares and keeps walking.

Once they are gone, Jetstorm emerges from the back room and peeks outside again.

"Your master and my brother-in-arms have

been captured, Russell Clay!" Jetstorm whispers to Russell. "The ones we thought to be Bumblebee and Grimlock must have been… Decepticons in disguise! We must escape! Climb onto my back and hold tight."

With Russell clinging to him, Jetstorm slips out the diner's back door and begins hopping, ninja-like, from junk pile to junk pile toward the exit.

On the way, they spot Foxtrot carrying a struggling Fixit toward the stasis pod controls. Jetstorm and Russell want nothing more than to help their teammates, but they know they are no match for Decepticons on their own.

Once they are safely outside the scrapyard, the pair hunker down in the woods.

"This isn't right, Jetstorm," Russell pleads. "I have to go back and rescue my dad!"

"I understand, Russell Clay," Jetstorm responds. "But we need help. We need to find Master Drift! Er, and the other bots."

Jetstorm attempts to contact Bumblebee on his wrist communicator, but he only hears static.

Without a message or a map, Russell climbs onto Jetstorm's back once again and the two of them head off in the same direction as their friends, hoping to intercept them in transit.

Back inside the scrapyard, Stilts over-turns an old shark-diving cage to form a makeshift prison for Denny and Slipstream.

"This should keep you out of my gears for now," the Decepticon remarks.

Foxtrot turns to Fixit and points a sharp claw at the Mini-Con. "Release the Ronin," he commands.

Fixit refuses to unlock Forager's stasis pod.

"No pay…ray…way!"

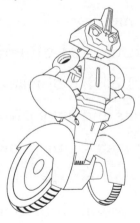

Furious, Foxtrot pulls out a blaster and aims it at the captives.

"I'm feeling a little rusty and could use the target practice!" he sneers.

The twitching Mini-Con reluctantly complies, too nervous to protest again. After a few keystrokes, Forager's cell slips open with a hiss and a pop.

"Ah, whatta nap!" Forager says, stretching and yawning. "I knew I could count on you fellas to spring me."

Forager, Foxtrot, and Stilts exchange an overly complicated handshake with lots of quick movements and jerky jabs.

"Ronin take care of their own, Forager," Foxtrot says, stuffing the no-longer-useful Fixit into the prison with Slipstream and Denny.

"It's funny you guys should mention that,"

Forager replies, popping a lockpick out of his finger and picking absentmindedly at his shiny metal teeth. "Right before I got pinched and stuffed in that cooler, I saw an old buddy palling around with these Autobots. Remember Deadlock? He was that samurai-bot, real into honor and stuff."

Foxtrot and Stilts both look stunned.

"I thought that bot got blasted on the moon of Athena," Foxtrot says.

"Yeah, no one ever saw him after that," Stilts adds, thinking back to that fateful mission. "We figured he was spare parts for sure."

"Well, if he was spare parts, someone sure put him back together well—and slapped an Autobot logo on him as a finishing touch," Forager replies.

The Ronins' trip down memory lane is short-lived, however, as Foxtrot's keen audio receptors pick up the sounds of Bumblebee, Strongarm, Sideswipe, and Grimlock attempting to sneak back into the scrapyard.

"The Autobots have returned, brothers," Foxtrot informs his fellow mercenaries. His face twists into garish grin. "Shall we escape or take this place over as our new base on Earth?" Stilts and Forager let out wicked cackles.

"As if that was even a question!" Stilts exclaims. "This'll make the perfect hideaway while we plunder and pillage as we please!"

"Sounds peachy, Foxtrot, but it's still three versus four, and I don't like them odds,"

Forager reminds him. "I ain't goin' back in that freezer."

"Don't worry, I think I have an old holocloak in my records that'll make this fight a lot more interesting...." Foxtrot replies with a sly smile.

The Decepticon punches a few codes into the display screen on his tail and two small discs pop out. He sticks one to his chest and pockets the other. "I'll save this hologram disc as a surprise."

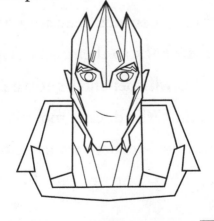

With a press of a button, Foxtrot dons a perfect hologram of Drift or—as they knew him—Deadlock!

"How do I look?" he asks.

"Like a sight for sore optics," Forager replies.

Across the scrapyard, Bumblebee and the

others walk nervously toward the diner with their blasters drawn.

As they turn a corner, they see Drift standing with their back to them.

Bumblebee whisper-shouts to their cryptic colleague, but Drift doesn't move or respond.

The Autobot leader walks closer...and closer...reaching out to put his hand on

Drift's shoulder when—*WHOOSH!*—it goes straight through!

"It's a hologram!" Bumblebee shouts to the others—a moment too late.

A second, solid "Drift" leaps out from behind a stack of cars and pins Grimlock to the ground.

"This is an ambush!" the pretend-Drift yells.

Before the big Dinobot can pummel his opponent, he is shocked with an electrical charge.

ZZZARK!

Sideswipe and Strongarm hurry to help their fallen friend, but Stilts and Forager appear and grab them by the wrists.

With a quick spin, the Ronin throw the

two young cadets into each other, knocking them both out!

WHAM!

As pretend-Drift and his allies tie up Bumblebee's teammates, the Autobot leader dashes behind a scrap pile and calls for help.

"Mayday, mayday!" he yells into his communicator's open channel. "Drift and his Decepticons have attacked the scrapyard. If anyone is left, send help!"

"Sorry, little guy," the disguised Foxtrot says, leaning over Bumblebee's hiding spot with Forager and Stilts behind him. "Those nice big wings of Stilts's block signal transmissions. You just spent your last moments of freedom sending out static."

The villains laugh and quickly pile on

Bumblebee, overpowering the struggling hero. Soon, Team Bee is dragged to the stasis pods. As quickly as they were captured, the Autobots are locked away and the Ronin are left in charge of the scrapyard!

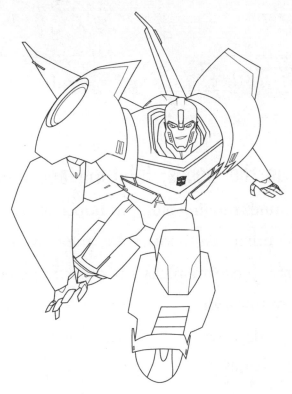

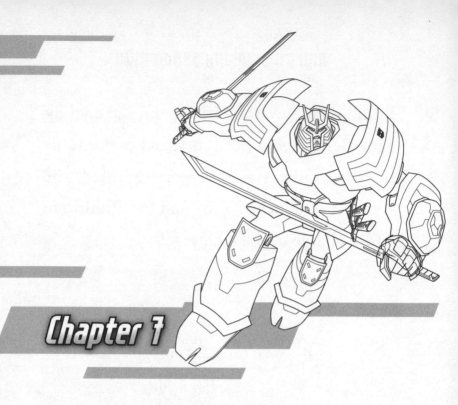

Chapter 7

Out in the woods, Jetstorm and Russell continue trudging along in hopes of running into other Autobots. As they near the quarry, Jetstorm picks up on a fragmented communication:

"Mayday, mayday…Drift…attacked…scrapyard…help!"

"Hey, that's Bumblebee's voice!" Russell says. "But that means Strongarm must have been right—Drift really is a traitor!"

Just as Russell puts Jetstorm's worst fears into words, the two of them look up to see Drift speeding toward them from across the quarry!

"Run!" Russell shouts at Jetstorm.

Jetstorm reluctantly complies, and the young boy hangs on tight as the Mini-Con sprints through the branches.

The roar of Drift's motor gains on them.

VROOOM!

Jetstorm bounces off trees left and right, cutting into a denser part of the forest. Together with Russell, he hides under a big, overturned tree trunk.

Suddenly, a large shadow passes overhead and lands in front of them.

It's Drift!

Russell and Jetstorm scream.

"Why do you flee from your master?" Drift booms, making Jetstorm shrink down on himself.

The Mini-Con may be easily intimidated, but Russell is not. The human climbs off Jetstorm's back and confronts Drift.

"Because you betrayed us!" Russell shouts.

He beats his fists on the cold metal exterior of Drift's shin. "You and your *real* team kidnapped my dad!"

Drift is instantly taken aback. "My 'real team'?" he asks.

"The Decepticons!" Russell yells. "The tall

one with wings and a beak and the mean-looking orange one with the big tail."

Drift's normally calm exterior breaks. He bends down and puts one massive hand around Russell's back to comfort him.

"Russell Clay, I did not attack the others, but I think I know who did," Drift says to the distraught young boy. "You must believe me if we are to rescue them."

Russell looks up into Drift's face, unsure

of what to do, but Jetstorm slowly walks over and kneels in front of Drift.

"I trust you, master," Jetstorm says, eyes averted.

Drift looks at him for a moment.

"Stand, student," he says. "I have not earned your trust. It is time that I come clean about my past. I had hoped to put it behind me, but I see now that my silence has put others at risk."

Drift shifts back into his sleek vehicle mode and opens the door for Russell to get in. Jetstorm takes his place on Drift's side.

Driving back to the scrapyard, Drift explains how he came to know the Ronin.

"Many cycles ago, Cybertron was a very different place," he begins. "When the

Decepticon movement first began, it wasn't clear how evil they were. They spoke about equality and political reform on Cybertron. It was easy to get swept up in all the talk, especially if you started life as a homeless bot stealing Energon just to survive. The skills I learned on the streets drew the attention of Megatron, the leader of the Decepticon movement."

Russell's jaw drops at the mention of Megatron. He's been around the bots long enough to know that Megatron means serious trouble.

"Megatron brought me in, gave me a purpose—and a new name: Deadlock." Drift continues. "I worked alongside the Decepticons for many cycles, watching the movement

grow increasingly destructive and distanced from its original goals. I did many things I am ashamed of, and for which I can never atone. When I was nearly destroyed in battle, a group of peaceful bots called the Circle of Light repaired me and allowed me to live among them, trading unending conflict for honor and self-control."

Drift sighs, sifting back through painful memories.

"Eventually the war reached even the Circle of Light, and my peace was shattered. For countless cycles after that, I wandered aimlessly, a samurai without a master or a cause. Which is exactly what the Ronin were looking for."

Drift rolls to a halt in the trees surrounding the scrapyard.

"What you must understand about the Ronin is that they answer to no one. Like me, they were Decepticons who grew disenchanted with Megatron's goals. There were many of them, and no single leader. They accepted me without questioning my past deeds. It was…comforting. But in time, I discovered that what they did, they did without honor."

"What did they do?" Russell asks nervously.

"They are bounty hunters, but they recognize no code of virtue. During my final job with them, a group of us followed a bounty to the moon of Athena, a distant planet with a large native population. The target retreated to a sealed bunker deep under the moon's surface. Rather than retreat, one of the Ronin, Foxtrot, suggested blowing the moon apart from space. The explosion would have been devastating to the inhabitants of the planet below."

Russell gasps.

"So what *did* you do?"

"The only thing I could," Drift replies. "When our ship neared bombing range, I set off a small explosion that scared everyone else into the ship's life pods. After they were clear, I triggered the rest of the explosives and then escaped myself. Our ship detonated in orbit. The Ronin were stranded in space until other members of the guild could rescue them, but I fled…determined to follow my path alone, and *with* honor."

His tale done, Drift shifts back into robot mode, letting Russell out first.

Jetstorm again kneels before his master.

"I trust you, master," Jetstorm says.

Drift bows to him.

"I trust you, too, student," Drift responds. "And you, Russell Clay of Earth. Now I ask that you maintain that trust. It will not be easy to defeat the Ronin that have captured your—our—friends. We will need to deceive them."

Drift, Jetstorm, and Russell approach the entrance of the scrapyard. The bright afternoon sun has set, giving the normally welcoming front gate a sinister vibe. A bot that appears to be Grimlock immediately greets them.

"Hello, big bot, small bot, and soft bot,"

pretend-Grimlock says in his dumbest voice. "Me am your Dinobot friend! It am safe to come inside."

"I do not think so, *Stilts*," Drift says, a serious look set on his face. "That is you under there, is it not?"

Pretend-Grimlock frowns and drops his holographic disguise.

"I thought Forager had brain rust when he told us he saw you, Deadlock," Stilts replies. "But it must be *you* with a malfunction if you've allied yourself with these pathetic Autobots."

Without warning, Drift snatches an unsuspecting Russell in one hand and pins Jetstorm to the ground with the other.

"You mean these two?" Drift asks. "I was just tracking down the strays. The Decepticons have a sizable standing bounty for these bots, and I mean to collect."

"Is that so?" Stilts asks, not quite believing Drift's story. "Forager said you seemed pretty chummy with them when he got locked up."

"Do you know of an easier way to capture this many bots solo?" Drift responds without missing a beat. "I was about to start picking them off when Forager blew my cover. Now let me in and we'll discuss how we are going to split the payday."

Stilts still looks unconvinced.

"A nanocycle ago I thought you were nothing but debris drifting through space in a galaxy far, far away," Stilts says. "You're going to have to talk to Foxtrot before I trust anything that comes out of your speech module."

"Oh, is Foxtrot your leader now?" Drift challenges.

"The Ronin have no leader," Stilts says through an angrily clenched beak. "We take care of our own."

The tall Decepticon reluctantly lets Drift in with his struggling prisoners.

When they pass the makeshift holding cell, Drift roughly tosses Russell and Jetstorm inside. Russell just catches the slightest hint of a wink as the former bounty hunter leaves them locked up.

Inside the command center, Foxtrot and Forager are flipping through the prison transport records, taking note of which other members of the Ronin were on board when the ship crashed on Earth. Foxtrot isn't happy to see Drift.

"Shouldn't you be in stasis, traitor?" Foxtrot hisses, flexing his claws.

"Whoa, whoa, wait-a-minute, tough guy," Forager interrupts, putting himself between Foxtrot and Drift. "I'm sure our old pal Deadlock—or should I say *Drift*—has a solid explanation for why he's here and how he's still in one piece."

"There is not much to say," Drift states in his typically stoic fashion. "Our ship went down. I thought *you* blew up. You thought *I* blew up. I work alone now. End of explanation."

"You work alone *until now,* right, old buddy?" Forager says, chuckling.

He wraps a thick arm around Drift's shoulders. "This is fate! We're getting the gang back together. With all them stasis pods and fancy equipment, we can sell the Autobots to the Decepticons and the Decepticons to the Autobots. We'll be rich!"

The cunning crook cackles at his own idea.

"We'll be richer if we don't split the bounties with this backstabber," Foxtrot growls.

"And how long will you waste learning about this equipment and this planet?" Drift asks. "These foolish bots taught me everything."

"Did they teach you how to use the trash

compactor?" Stilts asks. "We were just brainstorming fun ways to deactivate the Mini-Cons. No bounty on those runts."

Drift's face remains calm and unreadable.

"No, but I do know the locations of all the Energon caches they've discovered," Drift says.

The Ronins' optics go wide.

"And we'll need more Energon to power the locators and track down the rest of the bounties," Drift adds. "I've been itching for some action after holding back around these law-bots. Anybot who wants to join me is welcome to follow."

Stilts and Forager look at each other and grin. These rough-and-tumble Decepticons are always up for causing a mess. Foxtrot doesn't hide his distrust of Drift, but he reluctantly joins along.

On the way out of the scrapyard, Forager stops to taunt the prisoners.

"Enjoy the scenery while it lasts, you byte-sized bots," Forager says, rattling the makeshift cage containing Denny, Russell, and the Mini-Cons. "When we come back, we're gonna have fun recycling you."

Drift stands idly by while the Ronin harass his former charges.

When Forager grows tired of the game, they all shift into their vehicle forms and roll out.

Forager turns into a Cybertronian dirt buggy, Foxtrot becomes a sleek alien sports car, and Stilts takes flight as an otherworldly jet plane.

Drift—or, rather, Deadlock—leads the way in his Earth car mode.

Once they are alone, Russell helps his dad

to his feet and turns to Jetstorm with a nervous look on his face.

"So this is still all just an act, right? Drift hasn't betrayed us for real?" Russell asks.

"We will soon find out," the Mini-Con replies.

Chapter 9

"Where are we headed, Deadlock?" Stilts
asks, soaring through the air above the other
three bots. "Maybe we can try out the old
bomb-from-above move again—get it right
this time!"

"No need," Drift replies. "The last Decepticon those do-gooders captured hid his stash

in an auto factory that should be deserted at this time of night. The native population does not understand Energon, so there was no risk of them stealing it for themselves."

Foxtrot banks a hard turn to the right, fender-checking Drift and nearly pushing him off the road.

"A deserted factory?" Foxtrot growls angrily. "I thought you were taking us someplace we could cut loose and have some fun. If

I wanted to just have a peaceful picnic, I'd have stayed in the woods."

Drift revs his motor and pulls ahead, kicking up dirt and rocks that bounce off Foxtrot's windshield.

"There is no sense in exposing our existence to the humans until we are at full strength," Drift replies curtly.

He grinds to a halt in front of an imposingly large factory, set off from main roads and the general populace of Crown City. The sun is down, and all the factory workers are home for the night.

The Ronin switch back into their bot modes, ready to rampage and nab some Energon.

"We'll scale the exterior and enter through the skylight," Drift says."

"No can do, old pal. This bot doesn't climb," Forager says, pointing to himself. "I ain't no good unless I got both paws planted firmly on the ground. Let me take care of this."

The crafty crook pops a lockpick out of his claw to open the large delivery bay doors. Before he can finish tinkering with the lock, Foxtrot steps forward, pulls out his blaster, and shoots a hole through the door.

BLAM!

"Oops," he says sarcastically. "Trigger digit slipped."

"Get a load of this bot, will ya?" Forager

says, slapping Foxtrot on the back. "That's why they call him the Trigger-Happy Terror!"

"That's not what *I* call him," Stilts replies with a smirk.

Foxtrot flashes his teeth at his comrade. "Quit grinding my gears," he snarls.

"Ah, shove it down your intake valve," Stilts retorts.

The bots pile inside, towering above the human-sized proportions.

Stilts's cranium grazes the factory ceiling.

"You know, maybe I better wait outside," he says. "I'm not a big fan of tight spaces."

Foxtrot gives the bot a shove to keep moving and stop complaining.

Drift leads the Ronin to a decommissioned part of the factory, blocked off with yellow caution tape. They smash through equipment and knock over auto parts as they walk along.

"I see you have mastered the art of stealth in my absence," Drift observes dryly.

He directs them toward a hulking tarp-covered shape and pulls the cover off.

The Decepticons have discovered a gargantuan, glowing stack of Energon cubes—ripe for the taking!

"Well, hello, beautiful!" Forager squeaks.

They each grab as many cubes as they can carry and turn to leave the way they came in.

As they near the exit, Drift is the first to spot a human security guard at the far end of a long hallway. The man is inspecting the smoldering remains of auto parts the Decepticons trashed on their way in.

"This is Officer Wong," the man whispers into a walkie-talkie. "I need to report a serious break-in and a *lot* of damage."

Foxtrot's audio receptors perk up. He turns toward the sound and spies the human.

"Perfect," Foxtrot says, whipping out his blaster. "Some target practice for ol' Trigger-Happy!"

The Decepticon takes aim, but Drift blocks his shot.

"You lack finesse, Foxtrot," Drift says. "*I* will handle this!"

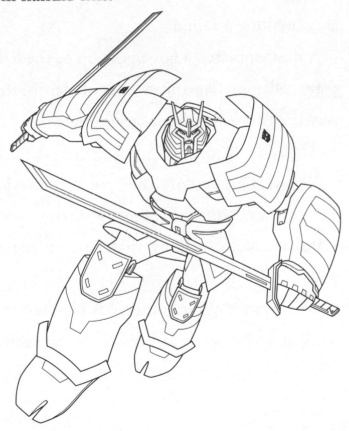

In a flash, Drift unsheathes his sword and spins gracefully through the air. With a blur of movement, his blade slices and dices the ceiling above them. Then he lands without even making a sound.

A moment later, a large portion of the hallway collapses, leaving a pile of debris that seemingly crushes the security guard.

THUD!

"Wow! This samurai has got some style," Forager exclaims. "These fleshbags don't stand a chance against that can opener of his!"

Foxtrot snarls and holsters his blaster.

Meanwhile, on the other side of the rubble, a perfectly unharmed and frightened Officer

Wong hightails it to his police cruiser and speeds away.

With their stashed Energon in tow, the bots hustle out the exit and shift into vehicle mode. Satisfied that their heist is complete, they blaze a trail back to the scrapyard.

Upon their return, the Decepticons dump

their loot near the captives. Their fluids are pumping from the caper, and they finally begin to let down their guard around Drift.

Reminiscing about their old days running the space ways together, Forager reenacts a particularly crazed fight. He waves his arms and fires his blaster all around.

"Then I tried to grease that gearhead's wheels, but he threatened to blow my gasket!" Forager says, finishing his story.

The crook laughs so hard he falls backward. His exhaust pipe starts to sputter and a noxious gas fills the air.

"Filth!" gasps Stilts, covering his beak. "That went right in my vents!"

Forager laughs even harder, and even Foxtrot manages to break a smile.

"Ah yes," says Drift, standing and drawing several *shuriken* from his waist. "I seem to remember bailing your bumper out using... these!"

He slings the throwing stars across the scrapyard, whizzing them through the bars of the jail.

The sharp, spinning blades barely avoid hitting Denny, Russell, and the Mini-Cons, all of whom duck and recoil in fear.

The Ronin laugh uproariously and continue telling old battle tales as they wander off down another corridor.

Once the Decepticons are out of sight, Russell checks out something tied to one of the *shuriken*.

It is a note that reads: *Go now. Release the others.*

Russell shows the note to his fellow captives, a slow smile dawning on each of their faces.

Drift is not a traitor after all!

Slipstream checks the bars near where the *shuriken* entered and realizes that his master had discreetly sliced through the cage door, opening a space large enough for everyone to climb out!

Quickly and quietly, the five escapees slink toward the command center.

Upon reaching the control console, Fixit rapidly types away, and the stasis pods containing Bumblebee, Strongarm, Sideswipe, and Grimlock open up.

WHOOSH!

Bumblebee pops up and shakes the stasis freeze from his optics.

"Come on, team," he says, rallying the bots. "It's time to catch that Drift!"

Chapter 10

"Bumblebee, NO!" Russell shouts as the
Autobot leader shifts into vehicle mode. "It's
not what you think! Drift isn't a bad guy!"

"He could have fooled me," Bumblebee responds. "He led us straight into an
ambush."

"That wasn't Drift," Russell explains. "One of the Decepticons can make holograms. Drift was a part of their gang a long time ago, but he quit when they were going to hurt a bunch of people. Jetstorm and I helped Drift infiltrate them to rescue you!"

Bumblebee considers this new information.

"It looks like I might owe Drift an apology if we make it out of this," Bumblebee says. "But right now we need to act before their scanners notice we're out of stasis. Let's go help our teammate, Autobots!"

Team Bee tears through the scrapyard and quickly comes face-to-face with the Ronin outside the diner. Without pause, they all leap into battle!

Grimlock barrels his massive bulk at Stilts,

but the nimble bot immediately switches into his plane mode and flies out of reach. He fires at the Dinobot from up high. *CHOOM!*

Strongarm discharges her blaster at Forager, who scurries under a pile of old cars and tunnels out of reach.

"You ain't putting me back in that cell, law-bot!" Forager screams.

Sideswipe sets his sights on Foxtrot, the most deceptive of the Ronin.

The young Autobot flips through the air toward his target—only to smash right through a hologram instead! While Sideswipe regains his bearings, the real Foxtrot appears and delivers a painful blow.

"Flashy but not too bright," the Decepticon says.

As the rest of the team struggles against the Decepticons, Bumblebee dashes straight toward Drift. The samurai instinctively draws his sword.

"This is not as it appears, Bumblebee!" Drift shouts over the din of crashing metal. "I am not a traitor."

Bumblebee grinds to a halt right in front of the samurai-bot.

"I know, and I'm sorry for not trusting you earlier. Your past is behind you. But right now, we have a tough fight ahead of us, and we need to work together."

Bumblebee and Drift exchange curt nods. As Bee joins Sideswipe's fight against Foxtrot, Drift catches up with Grimlock.

The frustrated Dinobot is hurling cars up in the air at Stilts, with little success.

"Grimlock, catch!" Drift yells to the Dinobot, tossing him a small object.

Grimlock looks at the device in his hand.

"This tiny thing?" he exclaims. "I was having better luck with the cars."

"Trust me," Drift says.

The Dinobot winds his arm back and throws the device at the flying Ronin.

"One lob-ball special, coming up!" he announces.

Upon impact, the capsule becomes an expanding net like the one Stilts used to capture Slipstream and Denny.

The net tangles the Decepticon's wings and brings him down in a crash landing.

SMASH!

"Let me out of here! I hate tight spaces!" Stilts cries, twisting and turning on the ground.

"Better get used to it," Grim tells him. "Those stasis pods aren't exactly roomy!"

With Stilts dispatched, Drift and Grimlock sprint over to find Strongarm struggling with Forager, who has tunneled deep into a heap of junked cars. Every time Strongarm gets close, Forager fires his blaster left and right, covering the area.

Drift scans the area and sees the hydraulic lift machine.

"Strongarm, use that construction vehicle to remove his advantage!" Drift instructs her.

Strongarm, cautious to have confidence in Drift's loyalty, leaps behind the wheel of the large lift.

Pulling one lever, Strongarm swings the machine around and knocks over most of the stacked cars, exposing Forager's hiding spot. Then Strongarm flips on the powerful magnetic field, which catches Forager and drags the kicking and screaming Ronin high off the ground.

CLANG!

"Lemme go! Lemme go!" Forager yips. "I don't like heights!"

"Hang in there," Strongarm says smugly.

She joins Drift and Grimlock, and the trio race toward the fight against Foxtrot.

When they turn the corner, they find that Bumblebee and Sideswipe are not fighting the single remaining Ronin—they're tussling with over fifty Foxtrots!

"I know most of them are holograms, but the real Ronin keeps attacking us while we're distracted!" Sideswipe tells Drift, bringing him up to speed.

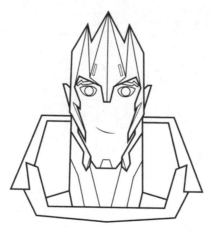

Drift thinks for a moment.

"Everybot stay calm and close your optics," Drift says.

"I thought you were on our side! Are you trying to get us blasted?" Strongarm asks.

"Do what Drift says, cadet!" Bumblebee orders. "Trust your instincts!"

The five Autobots stand totally silent, shoulder-to-shoulder and back-to-back. After a nanocycle of concentration, one noise breaks through the din of holographic humming: the clinking of Foxtrot unlatching his sidearm!

"There!" the bots all shout in unison.

Bumblebee, Strongarm, and Sideswipe point their plasma cannons and fire. The real Foxtrot takes three simultaneous hits and staggers back.

Projection discs crunch underfoot as Grimlock tramples across the scrapyard, extinguishing holograms left and right.

Foxtrot tries to make a break for it, but Drift gets a running start and tackles him to the ground.

"Ronin take care of their own," Drift says. "And you've been outfoxed."

He delivers a wallop of a punch right to Foxtrot's snout, laying him out flat!

POW!

Grimlock brings one massive foot down on the Ronin's tail, preventing him from crawling away.

"You may have defeated the Ronin, Deadlock," Foxtrot whispers, struggling under the Dinobot's weight. "But you can never change who you really are."

"There is no Deadlock, only Drift now," the reformed Autobot says.

"And *Drift* was never wicked like you to begin with," Bumblebee adds.

The Autobot leader turns toward Drift and reaches out his hand. "I apologize, Drift. I should have trusted you."

"Your apology is not necessary, Bumblebee," Drift replies, shaking his hand. "I did not trust you all with my past, and it became a danger to us. It is not in my nature to be so...open...but I vow to do better."

The Autobots help carry the rest of the bad

bots back to the stasis pods, where Russell, Denny, and the Mini-Cons are waiting.

Drift bows before Slipstream and Jetstorm.

"I humbly seek your forgiveness, students," he says.

Jetstorm and Slipstream look at each other, unsure of how to respond. They bow in return.

"We humbly grant it, master," the Mini-Cons reply in unison.

"Even though I am your master, I am still learning as well," Drift says quietly. "Today I have learned the virtue of trust, and that running from your past will only leave you to confront it alone and unprepared."

Grimlock surprises Drift with a big Dino-bot embrace.

"Welcome back!" he cheers.

"It is also not in my nature...to be so... close," grunts Drift.

The Autobots laugh and congratulate one another on another mission accomplished.

"I guess we do make a great team after all," Bumblebee says to Drift.

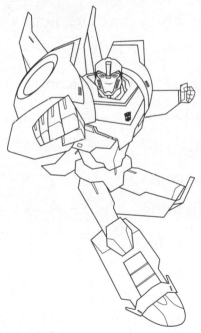

"And *you* make a great leader, Bumblebee," Drift replies. He bows to the yellow Autobot commander.

Bumblebee returns the gesture.

Drift helps his teammates load Foxtrot, Forager, and Stilts into stasis. As the pods slide shut, locking away the Ronin criminals, Drift can feel his past as Deadlock disappear with them.

He is no longer a Decepticon, a masterless samurai, or a Ronin fighting only for himself. He is an Autobot, fighting for Earth…and for his new friends!

The Trials of
Optimus Prime

The Trials of Optimus Prime

by John Sazaklis & Steve Foxe

A massive red-and-blue semitruck barrels through a narrow canyon, sounding its booming horn like a rallying cry.

Three other vehicles race close behind: a boxy blue police cruiser, a sleek red sports car, and a compact yellow coupe with black stripes.

At the opposite end of the canyon, an army of imposing figures stands armed and ready to fight. The semitruck and its convoy spit clouds of dust into the air as spinning wheels tear across the sandy ground.

Moments before the truck collides with the edge of the army, its wheels leave the ground, its shape twists and changes in the air, and it reveals itself to be much more than just a vehicle—it's actually a robot in disguise!

"Autobots, attack!" the robot shouts, landing so one massive foot crushes an enemy to the ground.

The three other vehicles follow suit, lifting into the air and changing into robot modes of their own!

The army of foes reveals itself to be

composed of snarling, angular robots of a much more sinister variety: Decepticons. These terrible foes brandish wicked blades and maces.

The four Autobots stand together as a team, pushing back attackers and knocking them off one by one with energy blasters and swords. The red-and-blue leader calls the shots and looks out for his teammates.

"Bumblebee, on your left!" the leader warns, directing the yellow-and-black bot to block an incoming blow.

CRASH!

The parried Decepticon staggers back and takes out a few of its brethren as it falls.

"Sideswipe, take out that cannon!"

The nimble red bot catapults over a pile

of rocks and slices through a pair of foes readying a massive energy cannon.

THUD!

The cannon hits the canyon floor and blasts back a whole fleet of Decepticons.

CHOOM!

"Strongarm, create a perimeter for us!"

VROOM!

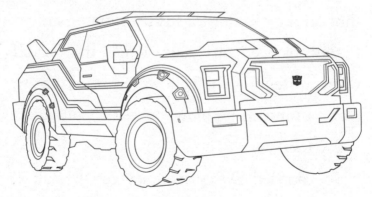

The broad-shouldered blue bot changes back into her vehicle mode and plows through the Decepticons, clearing a space for the Autobots to make a unified stand.

The enemies continue to swarm, but the four Autobots work together like one well-oiled machine.

"Good job, Autobots! But this Decepticon horde doesn't seem to be getting any smaller. We need backup."

With a flick of his wrist, the Autobot leader summons an energy shield to hold off the aggressive attackers. He speaks into the communicator embedded in his other arm.

"Fixit, we could use some extra feet on the ground right about now!"

The communicator crackles and hisses.

As if on cue, a shape darkens the sky above

the Decepticon infantry. Its shadow grows as it plummets toward the ground.

BOOOOOM!

The formidable figure smashes into the gathered Decepticons, flattening the unlucky enemies caught beneath it. The impact emits a shockwave that knocks many more off their feet.

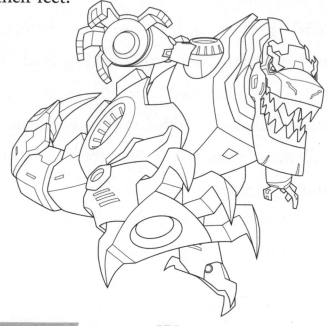

"Thanks for dropping in, Grimlock," the leader quips.

A huge black-and-green Dinobot climbs out of the crater he just formed, grins, and joins the rumble.

"Any time!" he replies, stampeding through the horde.

The leader can't help it: He cracks a smile, too.

Even as the enemy army doubles, then triples in size, he is confident that his team can stand strong against the forces of evil! He continues to bark orders and provide covering fire while countless Decepticons pour into the canyon.

Then, out of nowhere, a large swell of new enemies separates the huddled

Autobots. The leader can no longer watch his teammates' backs. He hears a pained cry ring out and then get cut short.

"Sideswipe!"

The red bot has fallen and is quickly covered by Decepticons.

Then another scream echoes through the canyon.

"Strongarm, no!" Optimus cries.

The blue police-bot drops against the canyon wall and is similarly overtaken.

The leader's resolve begins to crack, and the confidence he felt mere moments ago leaves him. He searches through the crowd for his remaining teammates. It's not too late to rally and force the Decepticons back....

A deep groan and an earthshaking thud tell him that the large Dinobot has been defeated, too.

Beating back Decepticons on every side, the leader pushes through to the yellow-and-black bot's position. Blades slice and maces smash against his plating as he prioritizes the search for his last standing teammate over his own safety.

Cannons fire around him into the canyon walls, throwing dust and rock shards into the air. Optimus hears a familiar cry and sees a blur of yellow fall toward the ground.

"Bumblebee!" the leader shouts. With a wide swoop of his sword, he knocks back a swarm of enemies to reveal the crumpled shape of the last remaining member of his team.

"No, not you, too," he whispers, kneeling beside his friend. The yellow-and-black bot barely moves.

"Optimus…" Bumblebee struggles to speak.

The leader looks down at his injured comrade.

"Optimus, the others…"

The dazed Decepticons pick themselves up and surround the duo. Escape is impossible.

The Autobot leader, Optimus, is soon covered on all sides, stumbling under the combined weight of his faceless assailants.

He struggles and strains to hear what Bumblebee has to tell him over the din of the Decepticon army.

And suddenly, the message is clear:

"Optimus...you failed us!"

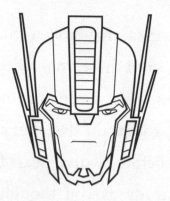

Chapter 2

For a few nanocycles, everything is dark. Then, one by one, the Decepticons piled on top of Optimus blink out of existence, like the static hum of a television set when it is unplugged.

The defeated Autobots are the only ones left in the canyon.

Optimus eyes the broken frames of his teammates, until those, too, fade away.

The leader looks down into his arms just in time to catch the last hazy shadow of Bumblebee before he disappears from sight.

"Not as ready as you thought you were, eh, hotshot?"

A voice rings out from the canyon walls above.

The next time it speaks, it comes from a different direction. "Hate to be so hard on you, but taking it easy never helped anyone."

Optimus squints up into the harsh light, searching for the source of the voice.

"Down here, big guy," the voice says, suddenly appearing behind the Autobot.

The voice's owner is a short green bot with bulky shoulders and a wide, square jaw. He hovers cross-legged a few feet off the canyon floor.

As he speaks, the canyon walls start to dissolve in a flurry of light, until the space around the two bots becomes a vast, nondescript void.

"My teammates…" the leader mumbles, as if waking up from a dream.

"Not your *real* teammates, Optimus, just holograms of bots you barely know," the floating figure replies. "Except for that yellow one, I guess. And *maybe* I went too far by giving it dialogue processors."

Optimus narrows his optics.

"Those bots are Bumblebee's teammates. That makes them my allies. And I couldn't save them."

The green bot chuckles.

"Well, they're still holograms. Just like all the Decepticons who whooped your rear bumper. Not that it makes your new dents and scratches feel any better, I'm sure."

Optimus surveys the damage he accumulated during the simulated battle.

Despite the seemingly sharp weapons of the holographic Decepticons, his wounds are no more than surface-deep. The simulation wasn't meant to actually harm Optimus, only to test him.

The other bot waves his hand and a

shimmering light passes over Optimus, fixing any signs of damage.

"Thank you, Micronus," Optimus says, slightly bowing his head in respect. "The Realm of the Primes is still so disorienting to me. I know I am here to train and prepare myself for the battle ahead, but these simulations feel so real...."

"Would they do you any good if they didn't?" Micronus shoots back.

Micronus is one of the Thirteen, the

original Transformers created by Primus to battle Unicron eons ago. Each was designated a Prime and given unique powers and abilities.

Micronus is the very first Mini-Con, a race of small Cybertronians imbued with the ability to enhance the powers of their allies.

Ever since Optimus Prime made the ultimate sacrifice to restore the AllSpark to their home planet of Cybertron, he has existed in the Realm of the Primes. Here, he strengthens himself physically and mentally for an ominous and unknown battle to come. Micronus has served as his mentor...and he hasn't gone easy on his pupil.

"Now shake it off. We're far from done here," Micronus says.

"I need to return to Earth," Optimus replies. "Every day that passes is another day that the Decepticons could strike. Bumblebee and the others need me."

Micronus scrutinizes his student.

"Do they need you, or do you need *them*?"

Optimus doesn't respond.

"Pellechrome wasn't built in a millennium,"

Micronus says. "And you just royally scrapped that training sequence. I'm not exactly shooting confidence in your abilities out of my tailpipe right now."

"I understand your reservations, Micronus," Optimus replies. "But I've faced Megatron. I've stood against Unicron. And now it's time for me to rejoin my team on Earth."

"You're serious, aren't you?" Micronus asks with a scoff. "All right, I'll convene with the other Primes to discuss this. No promises, though. You're still rough around the grill as far as I'm concerned."

Before Optimus can thank the elder bot, Micronus fades away in a glimmer of sparks, leaving Optimus alone in the Realm of the Primes.

An unknown distance away, Micronus reappears, hovering in the shadow of a council of immense bots: the Primes. Of these powerful beings, only Micronus has chosen to reveal himself to Optimus.

"Okay, fellas," Micronus says, comfortable among his brethren. "The kid is getting antsy. He wants to return to Earth."

A booming laugh breaks out among the shadowed Primes.

"He's bold enough to suggest that he is ready after failing against a mob of your conjured Decepticons?" a deep voice asks.

"'Bold' or 'stupid'?" a cackling voice chimes in.

Micronus turns toward its source.

"Optimus is far from stupid, Liege Maximo," he retorts. "He is one of our best chances at beating back the growing darkness. Not that I would expect *you* to care."

The figure with the deep voice speaks again to Micronus.

"You are right to believe in Optimus's potential, but he is not yet ready. We have been too easy on him, and his progress has faltered as a result. We charge you, Micronus, with making his training more rigorous. When he does return to Earth, he must be *prepared*."

"Your wish is my command sequence,

brothers," Micronus replies, fading away to give Optimus the disappointing news.

As the other Primes drift off, Liege Maximo remains. He pulls his cape around his frame and flexes the imposing hornlike appendages on his head.

"Perhaps I *should* care about Optimus's training...." Liege Maximo says aloud to himself, forming a plan. "After all, having a new plaything to manipulate might help relieve my boredom!"

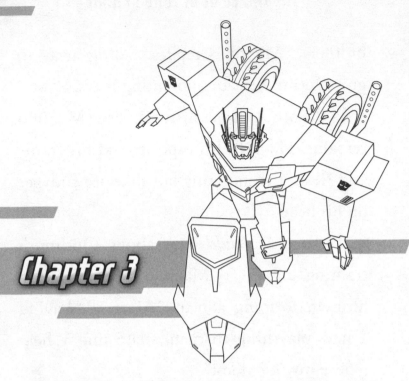

Chapter 3

"Well, don't act surprised," Micronus tells Optimus as the Autobot leader processes his disappointment. "We didn't bring you here for scraps and giggles, we brought you here to prepare to face unimaginable evil."

"Worse than Unicron and Megatron?"

Optimus asks. "Because I defeated them—*with* my team. I trust Bumblebee to protect Earth in my absence, but what if this great evil strikes before the Primes think I'm ready?"

Micronus hovers high above Optimus. He waves his hands and four large bots rise out of the ground. Each is outfitted with hefty shoulder cannons.

"You think you're ready? Prove it."

Optimus flexes his pistons.

"Bring on the slag-heaps!" he shouts.

"Oh, we're going to make things a little more interesting now," Micronus responds.

He lets out a laugh and waves his hand.

Glimmering buildings rise out of the ground, creating an approximation of a metropolis on Earth. With another wave of his hand, smaller holograms of humans appear.

"Think you can keep these little ones safe?" As soon as Micronus issues his challenge, the four weaponized bots split up and dart after different groups of the holographic civilians.

Optimus springs into action!

He chases after the biggest bot and leaps onto its back. Optimus unsheathes his energy sword and wedges it under the bot's shoulder cannon.

SHTICK!

The bot tries to shake Optimus loose, but Optimus uses all of his weight to pry the cannon loose from its shoulder mount.

With a backward leap, Optimus lands

with the cannon in one arm and holsters his sword.

Optimus tugs on the cannon's firing mechanism, blasting the big bot off its feet in a noisy explosion of energy.

CHOOM!

"One down, three to go!"

With one group of civilians safe, Optimus hoists the cannon onto his shoulder and aims it toward another adversary.

BOOM!

Optimus drops the cannon and darts after the remaining robots.

"Don't get cocky, Optimus!" Micronus shouts.

"Oh no, please *do* get cocky, Autobot," another voice whispers just out of audio receptor distance. "And reckless. It will be much more fun if you're reckless!"

Unbeknownst to Micronus and Optimus, they've got an unseen guest watching them: Liege Maximo!

Liege Maximo is not necessarily evil, but his petty jealousy and boredom motivate him to be a tricky troublemaker.

While Optimus chases down the third bot, Liege Maximo pulls the fourth one into an alley. He twitches his horns and reprograms the bot to be much more vicious in its attacks! He also installs a few surprises for Optimus.

His meddling accomplished, Liege Maximo slips away out of sight. He settles into a spot high up on one of the fake buildings where he can watch the chaos unfold unobserved.

Just then, Optimus subdues the third bot, saving the humans from being harmed.

"Last one! It's closing time!"

The brave Autobot leader dashes through the holographic streets, eager to find his final foe.

Before he can, a cannon blast knocks him off his feet and sends him flying into a nearby wall.

CRASH!

"Ouch! These simulations aren't playing around!"

Optimus climbs to his feet and rushes toward the source of the blast.

When the bot charges up for a second cannon blast, Optimus summons his energy shield.

The bot fires, but Optimus deflects the blast.

FWOOM!

The Autobot leader draws his sword and watches his attacker's arms suddenly turn into spinning saw blades!

"Saving the worst for last, Micronus?" Optimus asks under his breath.

Micronus is puzzled by this development.

"I may be many eons old," he says to himself, "but I'm pretty sure I didn't summon attack-bots with saw-blade arms...."

Meanwhile, Optimus pedals backward, stepping out of the path of the spinning blades.

The attack-bot presses forward, preparing to fire its cannon again!

Optimus pulls up his shield, just as a large

volley of energy—much larger than before—shoots directly at Optimus.

His shield splinters, but not before reflecting the bulk of the blast, aiming it back at the bad bot.

KABOOM!

When the dust clears, Optimus finds himself in the wreckage of one of the holographic buildings. He stumbles into the street and sees what's left of his opponent: a lone saw blade rolling across the pavement.

Optimus didn't survive unscathed, though. His injuries feel much more serious than before, as if this simulation was actually meant to hurt him!

Luckily, none of the simulated humans were in this part of the city. Despite the damage he sustained, Optimus feels good about his training session.

"Looking sharp, Optimus," Micronus says, hovering down to the Autobot's level. "Did you find this session...particularly challenging?"

Optimus doesn't want to admit to his mentor that he's actually hurt. If the Primes don't think he's mastering their tasks, they won't let him return to Earth. The Autobot leader grimaces through the pain.

"It was a pretty close shave, but nothing I couldn't handle."

Micronus is suspicious—not of his pupil's abilities, but of the attack drone's weapons.

Still, the drill is complete. He waves his hands, and the cityscape and its humanlike inhabitants fade away. A second gesture heals some of the dents and scrapes on Optimus's frame, but the deeper wounds inflicted by the fourth bot still ache.

As the last of the buildings fade away, Micronus thinks he spots something in one of the higher windows.

But as quickly as he notices it, it's gone.

A trick of the light, he thinks.

A moment later, some distance away within the expansive Realm of the Primes, Liege Maximo reappears. The wicked Prime laughs uncontrollably, pleased with himself for manipulating Micronus's training exercise with Optimus—and getting away with it.

He summons a crude mock version of the

Autobot leader. He throws his cape over his shoulder and begins to slowly pace away from the motionless mannequin.

"Optimus, Optimus, Optimus…so eager to prove yourself that you'll suffer through pain," Liege Maximo says aloud.

As he paces, he pulls a small handful of dangerously sharp darts out of a holster near his waist. "I suppose the one question left to answer…"

Liege Maximo spins on his heels and lets the darts fly. They embed themselves in the fake Optimus's head!

"…is just how much pain can you take?"

Chapter 4

Micronus leads Optimus through the Realm of the Primes. Although he doesn't mention it, Micronus notices that the Autobot leader is walking with a slight limp.

"It's not time for you to return to Earth, Optimus," Micronus says. "But that doesn't mean you can't check in on things."

Micronus stops at the base of a hill. He waves his hands in a familiar gesture and then urges Optimus to climb the hill. The Autobot leader does as instructed and finds a reflecting pool at the top. Through it, he can see Earth!

"I wouldn't count sheepbots for too long, but I think you earned a break," Micronus says, turning to give Optimus some privacy. "Consider it a reminder of whom you're fighting for."

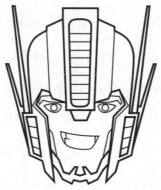

The Prime disappears, leaving Optimus alone with the portal.

As Optimus peers into it, his friends begin to come into view....

"Go long, Sideswipe!" Rusty Clay shouts, running backward and winding his arm up to throw a football.

"Let it rip, Rusty!" Sideswipe hollers, nimbly running through the junk-filled aisles of the scrapyard.

Rusty is the young son of Denny Clay, owner of the scrapyard that Bumblebee and his team of Autobots call home while on Earth.

Sideswipe was a bit of a troublemaker

back on Cybertron, but even though he has a bit of an authority problem, he's an invaluable member of the team.

Rusty lets the ball fly through the air. It tears through the sky in a perfect arc...until a pair of giant metal jaws chomp down on it, instantly deflating it!

"HOLE IN ONE!" Grimlock shouts, the now-useless rubber of the ball dangling from his open mouth.

Grimlock is a reformed Decepticon. What he lacks in common sense, he makes up for in strength, loyalty, and enthusiasm.

"Yeah, hole in one, all right—hole in the one lob-ball we had!" Sideswipe says, yanking the remains from Grimlock's teeth.

"That was a football, not a lob-ball, Sideswipe," Rusty says with a frown. "And 'hole in one' is from a different sport...."

"Don't feel bad, Russell Clay," Fixit says, patting Rusty on the back. "I can fit...flip... fix it right up!"

Sideswipe hands the deflated ball to Fixit, the team's Mini-Con.

Fixit was the pilot of the *Alchemor* maximum-security prison transport ship that crashed on Earth, releasing Decepticon prisoners across the planet. The crash also damaged Fixit's speech modules, which is why he sometimes trims...tricks...trips over words!

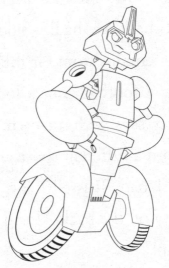

"That's okay, Fixit. I'm sure my dad has some 'vintage' footballs around here somewhere," Rusty says.

"Nonsense! I'll repair this in two nano-cycles."

Fixit shifts his hand into a complex drill tool.

Before Rusty can stop him, Fixit has somehow mangled the ball even worse.

"Oh my! This doesn't seem to have worked at all!"

Across the scrapyard, Bumblebee sits at the command center computers with Strongarm, his eager, law-abiding second-in-command. While the others play, Bumblebee and Strongarm use the computer's sensors to search for Decepticon fugitives roaming the area.

"Strongarm, why don't you go join the other bots?" Bumblebee suggests to his lieutenant. "It looks like our Decepticon pals are lying low today. You should relax a little."

"No, thank you, sir," Strongarm replies, straightening into a salute. "My place is at your side."

"I think you should take your place a little less seriously once in a while, cadet."

Strongarm frowns.

"How about this: I order you to go keep an eye on the others," Bumblebee says, approaching the request from a different angle. "And if you happen to have fun in the course of your mission, that's permissible."

Strongarm maintains a serious look on her face.

"Sir, yes, sir!"

Bumblebee shakes his head as the cadet exits the command center.

"Was I ever that eager with Optimus?" Bumblebee wonders aloud to himself.

Back in the Realm of the Primes, Optimus

smiles down at his former lieutenant.

"You certainly were, Bumblebee."

"Why aren't you ever that excited to see me?" Micronus asks, suddenly appearing in front of Optimus. Micronus gestures at the portal and it begins to close, cutting off Optimus's brief glance at his Autobot teammates on Earth.

"Bumblebee has assembled a good team

down there," Optimus says. "I don't know if he realizes it yet, but he has."

"I'm glad someone is adequately filling your stabilizers while you're away," Micronus says. "But it's time for you to reassemble and get some rest. I have new trials planned for you once you've recharged."

As Optimus limps away from the hill, following the hovering form of Micronus, a third figure slinks up to where the portal just closed.

"You're going to be even more fun than I had hoped, Optimus!" Liege Maximo whispers, horns twitching.

He waits for the two bots to clear the area and then repeats the gesture that Micronus made. Immediately, the portal reopens, focusing back on Bumblebee sitting at the computer console.

"It's showtime!"

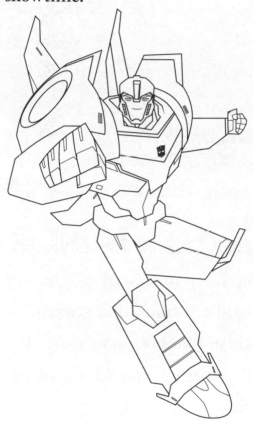

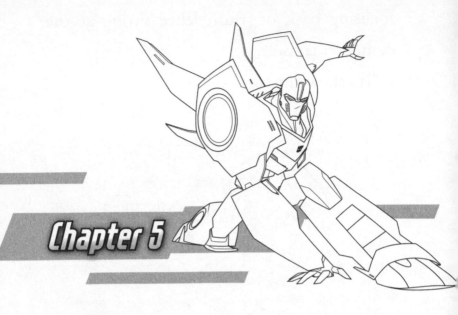

Chapter 5

Bumblebee taps at the keys, his optics growing weary from staring at facts and figures spread across multiple screens.

The other Autobots, now joined by Strongarm, are messing around elsewhere in the scrapyard.

The mysterious and stoic Autobot Drift, a

recent ally, is off on his own scouting mission with his two Mini-Cons, Slipstream and Jetstorm.

Denny Clay is in the diner he calls home, cataloging barbarian toys from the eighties that he purchased online.

Unbeknownst to Bumblebee, the scheming Liege Maximo is looking down on him from the Realm of the Primes, outside of normal space and time.

Liege Maximo delights in causing disruption, and he knows now that Bumblebee and Optimus hold a deep bond of respect for each other.

Summoning his powers of manipulation, Liege Maximo creates an image of Optimus on one of Bumblebee's screens. Bumblebee is so used to processing data that he doesn't think much of it.

"When did I pull up this profile of Optimus?" Bumblebee asks out loud to himself.

He attempts to click it away, but he can't find a way to dismiss the file. As his confusion mounts, a familiar voice echoes through the speakers.

"BUMBLEBEE!"

Bumblebee nearly topples backward!

Since Optimus awoke in the Realm of the Primes, he has occasionally appeared to Bumblebee to deliver messages of encouragement or warnings against danger. But showing up in Bumblebee's computer is a first!

"Optimus? You startled me!" Bumblebee says, calming down. "What's the glitch? Do we need to prepare for an attack?"

"YES, BUMBLEBEE!" the voice booms once more.

Bumblebee is nervous—this isn't like the previous visions he's received.

"YOU MUST PREPARE FOR A TERRIBLE ATTACK!"

The yellow Autobot shouts into his wrist

communicator for his team to assemble in the command center immediately. He turns back to the screen.

"What kind of attack, Optimus? From whom?"

"FROM ME!"

The image of Optimus begins to laugh terribly before turning to static. The speakers fuzz and shoot sparks across the floor.

Bumblebee is stunned silent.

Before he can process what just happened, the rest of his team pours into the command center.

"What's wrong, sir?" Strongarm asks, the first to Bumblebee's side.

"I...I saw..." Bumblebee can't think of a way to explain what he just witnessed.

When he first started seeing Optimus, his teammates weren't sure if they believed him or not. It wasn't until the Autobot leader appeared in full metal form to help them out that everyone accepted it.

There's no way they're going to believe Optimus just showed up to warn Bumblebee of an attack—from Optimus himself!

"What did you see, Bee?" Sideswipe asks, impatient to know what's going on.

"I saw…"

"Skinkbomb!" Fixit shouts, pointing at the

screen behind Bumblebee. "Our leader must have spotted Skinkbomb, the Decepticon demolitions expert. His radar blip just appeared on-screen!"

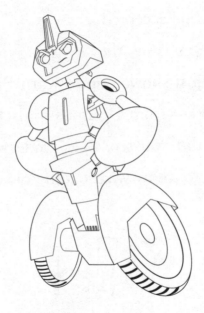

Fixit's treads roll across the floor to the console. His digits tip-tap across the keys and pull up a profile for Skinkbomb. The

Decepticon is broad and stocky, with reptilian features and a wide, squat tail.

Fixit chuckles to himself.

"No wonder Bumblebee is speechless—Skinkbomb has quite an ugly mug!"

"You got that right," Grimlock says. "And that tail don't look too pretty neither."

"Skinkbomb was apprehended for unauthorized demolitions on Cybertron," Fixit informs the group. "But he's explosive even without his bombs. His tail is actually a miniature warhead of its own, which he can detach at will and regrow by consuming metal and oil."

Strongarm looks expectantly at Bumblebee, who is still rattled by the sinister message from Optimus.

"Um, sir..." Strongarm says, nudging Bumblebee discreetly.

The Autobot leader realizes his team is staring at him.

"Oh, right," he mumbles. "Let's, um, get out there and...arrest...this Decepticon."

The other bots exchange puzzled looks. Their leader's lame attempt at trying to coin a catchphrase just now was especially pathetic.

"Wow," Sideswipe whispers to Grimlock. "Bee really dropped the lob-ball on that one, didn't he?"

Moments later, the Autobots are rolling out of the scrapyard.

According to Fixit's monitoring devices, Skinkbomb is at the base of the Crown City Bridge. Bumblebee and his team need to move fast to prevent catastrophe!

When they arrive, Strongarm, along with Denny and Rusty in police uniform disguises, head for the bridge's entrance to block oncoming traffic and clear the road of civilians.

Bumblebee leads Sideswipe and Grimlock under the bridge to confront Skinkbomb along the water's edge.

Strongarm, in police cruiser vehicle mode, uses her megaphone to help sell the urgency of the evacuation above. Within a few minutes, the bridge is cleared.

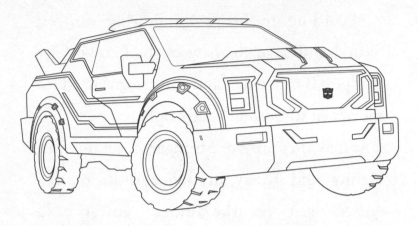

Rusty and Denny stay topside to maintain the barriers while Strongarm heads to the base of the bridge to join her teammates in a volatile battle.

KABOOM!

Skinkbomb is slow and bulky, but he is handy with explosives. Each time the Autobots gets close, Skinkbomb hurls a small grenade to keep them at a distance.

"Boom! You get an explosive! You get an explosive!" Skinkbomb vibrates with a deep, unhinged laugh. "I'll blow us all to bolts before I go back to lockup!"

Skinkbomb chucks a bomb toward Bumblebee, who dives out of the way in time to miss most of the blast.

The Autobot lands in the water below the

bridge. As he lifts himself out of the murk, a face slowly comes into focus through the rippling water.

"BUMBLEBEE!"

Bumblebee rubs his optics, convinced that it must be a trick of the water.

"I'VE SEEN THE ERROR OF MY WAYS, BUMBLEBEE," the vision of Optimus says to his former protégé. "ALIGNING OURSELVES WITH THE WEAK AUTOBOTS WAS A MISTAKE."

Bumblebee looks back at his team.

Grimlock, Sideswipe, and Strongarm are working together to get close enough to apprehend Skinkbomb, but the Decepticon is holding them off.

"What are you talking about Optimus? You're a hero!"

"I WAS A FOOL!" the voice bellows. "BUT NOW I AM STRONG."

Optimus's optics take on an eerie glow.

Bumblebee glances at his team once more as they struggle against their powerful foe. In battle against a dangerous Decepticon like Skinkbomb, every nanocycle counts!

He wants to go help them, but he's frozen in anticipation of what this vision of Optimus will say next.

"NOW...I AM A DECEPTICON!"

Chapter 6

The Autobot leader is distracted by his
vision of an evil Optimus.

"Watch out, Bee!" Sideswipe warns.

The agile young bot tackles Bumblebee,
pushing him out of the way of one of Skinkbomb's explosives.

BOOM!

Bumblebee gets slammed into a bridge support pillar by the force of the blast. His audio receptors are ringing, and his entire chassis is rattling. He is dinged up but otherwise unharmed.

But what about his teammate?

"Sideswipe!"

Bumblebee splashes through the shallow water to Sideswipe's side. The ninja-like Autobot is badly injured—having taken the brunt of the explosion while saving Bumblebee.

"Sideswipe, I need to get you out of here."

The battered bot struggles to speak.

"Don't sweat it, Bee…just take out…that Decepti…" Sideswipe's voice trails off.

Bumblebee props Sideswipe against a bridge support pillar and rushes back to the fight.

Grimlock and Strongarm are still dodging explosive blasts, seeking any opportunity to dash in and attack Skinkbomb.

When the dangerous Decepticon spots

a very angry and determined Bumblebee charging in his direction, he knows his luck is running out.

"Uh-oh, looks like it's time to bring the house down!"

The demolitions expert spins around and reveals that his bulbous tail is lighting up— the explosives within it are armed!

With a grinding of gears, the tail comes loose from Skinkbomb's frame.

"Hasta la vista, babies!" Skinkbomb shouts as he makes a break for it. "Exit, stage left!"

Bumblebee grinds to a halt a few feet from the tail.

Grimlock and Strongarm race after Skinkbomb, but their leader instructs them otherwise.

"There's no time, Autobots! Find cover, now!"

The flashing lights on the detached tail accelerate.

Team Bee runs toward the support pillars,

with its leader carrying Sideswipe over his shoulders.

The four Autobots duck behind the thick concrete just as—

BOOOOOOOOOM!

The force of the blast makes the bridge groan and sway.

Luckily, Strongarm and Grimlock were able to lead Skinkbomb far enough away that there is no structural damage.

Unfortunately, the explosion gave the Decepticon plenty of time to escape.

With an injured Autobot and no arrest, the mission is officially a failure.

The bots shift back into vehicle mode (and Grimlock into Dino mode), pick up the

Clays, and return to the scrapyard with their wounded comrade.

In the Realm of the Primes, Liege Maximo

cackles with delight. By briefly pretending to be Optimus, he has sown discord among the Autobots on Earth.

"They must think their fearless leader has brain rust!"

Pleased with himself, Liege Maximo closes the portal to Earth and travels through the Realm to check in on the *real* Optimus and his training under Micronus.

He finds the pair meditating atop two towering pillars.

"This doesn't look challenging *at all*," Liege Maximo whispers.

He uses his immense abilities to create a small fleet of sharp-limbed drone robots. Using their bladed arms, they quickly scurry up the pillars.

Without warning, the drones attack Optimus!

Before the Autobot can react, several of their blades slice against his frame, leaving painful rivets in the steel.

SLASH! SLASH!

"Micronus! Are you warning me never to let my guard down?"

Optimus summons his shield and unsheathes his sword.

The drones continue to leap at him with

thrashing claws. He blocks incoming blows and attacks back when he can, careful to maintain his balance atop the massive column.

Micronus is jarred out of his meditation by the clashing of blades. He looks across the divide between their pillars to find Optimus embroiled in battle against a small army of bladed assailants—bots he did not summon himself.

The pint-sized Prime rises from his position on the pillar. With one wave of his hand, he lifts Optimus up into the air. With another, he removes both pillars, sending the sharp little attackers plummeting. They smack into the ground, shatter into flecks of light, and disappear.

SKEESH!

Micronus lowers himself down and brings Optimus with him.

"I don't understand," Optimus says. "Did I perform the trial wrong?"

"No, Optimus," Micronus responds. "You weren't wrong—the attackers were. I didn't create those bots. Which means something is rotten in the Realm. Someone is interfering with your training."

Optimus looks around him for a likely

culprit, but the Realm of the Primes is an immense, shadowy place with an ever-changing landscape. Anyone wishing to hide would have plenty of places to do so.

"I need to convene with the rest of the Primes and discuss this troubling development."

Micronus creates a large, flat-topped pyramid out of the ground.

"You stay here. I don't want you caught by surprise until we find out who's behind this."

Optimus climbs to the top of the pyramid, where he can see most of the land around him.

"Micronus, are the other Primes testing me, too? I...I don't want to fail them."

"If they were, I'd know," Micronus replies.

"And wrecking you here wouldn't do us any good back on Earth or Cybertron."

Micronus points to Optimus's very real dents and scratches when he says this.

The Prime disappears, leaving Optimus alone.

Far in the distance, Liege Maximo grins wickedly, excited that his new plaything is all his for the moment!

Back on Earth, Strongarm and Grimlock help Bumblebee load Sideswipe onto Fixit's repair table. The brash young Autobot is badly banged up and is drifting in and out of rest mode.

"I've got him from here, Bee," the Mini-Con

says cheerfully. "Nothing some elbow grease can't fix! And some Energon infusions. And an extensive diagnostic repair kit—"

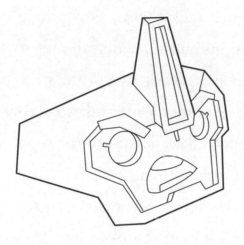

"We get it, Fixit," Bumblebee interrupts. "Just make sure he's okay, all right? It's my fault he's injured. I was distracted, and Sideswipe saved me from getting hurt by taking the blast himself."

Grimlock and Strongarm look away.

They're not used to their leader expressing this kind of regret.

"I want you two to stay by his side," Bumblebee tells them. "I'm going to track down Skinkbomb's whereabouts so we can put that dangerous dynamite stick back on ice." The Autobot leader takes another look at Sideswipe and walks out of the repair center.

"Grimlock, did you see what distracted Bee during the fight?" Strongarm asks.

"Uhh...it kind of looked like he was staring at his own reflection," Grimlock replies. "I like to look at my handsome face, too, but there's a time and a place, ya know?"

Fixit eavesdrops on Strongarm and Grimlock's conversation while he works away at repairing Sideswipe.

"Was Bumblebee acting dazed and confused without rear…fear…I mean, clear reason?" he asks.

Strongarm and Grimlock consider for a second, then respond in unison, "Yes."

"Have there been moments recently when

Bee seemed to be distant and aloof, as if he were in his own world?"

Strongarm and Grimlock think about it again, remembering Bee's odd behavior in the command center before the mission. They reply in the affirmative again.

"Ah, it's very simple, then," Fixit says. "Our leader must be suffering from brain rust!"

Chapter 7

Strongarm and the other members of Bumblebee's beleaguered team on Earth aren't the only bots grappling with concern for one of their own.

Back in the Realm of the Primes, Micronus again consults with his brothers about Optimus's training.

"You told me to take it harder on the kid, not turn him into spare parts," Micronus says, hovering in front of the shadowy figures of the Primes. "And if you entrust me to train him, you should let me know if you're going to stick your sprockets into the proceedings."

Micronus can't help a note of wounded pride from entering his voice.

"Has there been...an incident?" a deep voice asks.

Micronus looks at the Primes with mounting confusion.

"You mean to tell me you haven't been sending your own bots after Optimus?" the miniscule bot asks. "Real aggressive ones, loaded up with pointy blades?"

The gathered Primes look at one another for answers, but none claims responsibility.

"Wait a minute," Micronus says. "Where is he? Where is that no-good, horn-headed, backstabbing son of a slag-heap?"

The Primes step out of the shadows, revealing one fewer figure than the last time Micronus met with them.

"Where is Liege Maximo?"

Back at the pyramid, Optimus takes advantage of his solitude to practice sword techniques. Time does not pass the same in the Realm of the Primes as it does on Earth or Cybertron, and the Autobot leader finds that he rarely needs to rest.

Optimus's desire for justice and peace has always been enough to drive him, but he misses working alongside his teammates.

Unfortunately, Liege Maximo has figured this out from watching Optimus check in on Bumblebee and the crew on Earth, and he hatches a diabolical idea.

With a stir of his horns and a wave of his

hands, the manipulative mischief-maker conjures up an approximation of Bumblebee, visually identical to the Autobot stationed back on Earth, except with a pair of creepy red optics.

Liege Maximo imbues the false bot with a devilish mean streak and directs it toward Optimus's pyramid!

His plan in motion and a smirk on his face, Liege Maximo gathers his cape and retreats to a safe viewing distance. He creates a curtain of fog to hide his presence.

"And now it's time for the second act!" he says.

In between thrusts of his blade, Optimus picks up on a slight noise, like treads scraping against the mysterious bedrock of the Realm. The red-and-blue hero glances around, noticing the gathered fog for the first time.

"You're not going to catch me off guard, Micronus!" Optimus shouts into the near-total silence. He swings around with his blade drawn…and comes face-to-face with Liege Maximo's cruel creation!

"Bumblebee?!"

Optimus is shocked at first, but remembers

Micronus's holograms of his teammates during the canyon simulation.

The Autobot leader is a fast learner and a quick thinker. A trick like this can't fool him for long!

"Did Micronus create you to test my emotions?" Optimus asks.

The fake Bumblebee rushes forward and grabs Optimus by the shoulders.

"I'm real, Optimus!" Bumblebee says. "And I'm here because we failed! Earth is lost!"

The Autobot leader staggers back out of the fake Bumblebee's grasp. His confidence that this isn't the Bumblebee he knows is slightly shaken.

"We couldn't stop what was coming without your help. Now the others are gone, and

I'm stuck here in this weird place with you," the false friend explains.

Optimus hesitates, but stands firm that the feeling in his bolts is true.

"I don't believe you," he says. "Tell me something that only Bumblebee would know, something that will prove to me that you're the bot I've trusted by my side in the past— and that what you're saying about Earth is true."

The imposter bot stares at Optimus.

Some distance away, Liege Maximo fumes with fury.

"Scrap! Curse that Optimus and his resistance to my trickery. I'll just have to use a little force!"

The Prime upgrades his creation to unnerve Optimus even more.

"Come on, buddy, you *know* it's me, deep in your spark," Bumblebee says, shaking the bigger bot's frame. "It's me...your ol' pal BEE!"

The evil imposter leaps at Optimus, red optics glaring.

With the back of his sword, Optimus clocks the phony Bumblebee in the noggin.

BONK!

"Is that how you treat an old friend?" the dazed doppelgänger whines.

Optimus unleashes a powerful roundhouse kick that sends Bumblebee tumbling off the pyramid. He slides down the side like a skater grinding a pipe, shooting up sparks as he goes.

By the time he reaches the bottom, the mock Bumblebee has faded away like the other constructs of the Realm.

The fog recedes and disappears, too.

"Micronus!" Optimus yells. "Micronus, what sort of test is this?"

"No test of mine, for Solus Prime's sake," Micronus says, suddenly appearing behind Optimus.

With an aggressive wave of his hand, the pyramid rapidly flattens.

"Optimus, we have a big problem, and his name is Liege Maximo."

Some distance away from Optimus and

Micronus, Liege Maximo continues to seethe.

"That humorless, rust-headed reject is ruining everything!" Liege Maximo says aloud to himself. "This realm is *endlessly* boring and the other Primes are no fun at all. Now the first new plaything to come along in eons is already growing wise to my tricks!"

The horned bot paces back and forth, considering his options.

In the midst of his stomping, Liege Maximo notices that he is near a small hill. He climbs the gentle slope and stares down into the pool at the top of it, the perfect plan leaping instantly into his manipulative mind.

"If Optimus won't play along, I'll turn my attention back to these other new toys."

With a wicked wave of his hand, the pool at Liege Maximo's feet stirs and reveals a window to another place, far away from the Realm of the Primes: the scrapyard on Earth, with the real Bumblebee and the other bots!

Chapter 8

Bumblebee enters the command center cautiously, remembering his vision of an unhinged Optimus. He doesn't want to believe that these garish glimpses of his former leader are real, but they certainly felt like they were....

Even if the visions were just hallucinations

brought on by stress and pressure, they threw Bumblebee off his game during the Autobots' battle with Skinkbomb. He takes full responsibility for the injuries Sideswipe sustained, and the only way to make it up to him is to track down the escaped Decepticon!

Bumblebee runs his digits over the keys of the computer console, bringing it to electronic life. He pulls up Fixit's tracking software and sets the radius as wide as it will go.

The outskirts of Crown City, where the team first fought Skinkbomb, are clear of Decepticon life-forms. The forest around the scrapyard is likewise deserted.

The quarry on the other side of the forest, however, shows one big red blip on the radar!

"Bingo!" Bumblebee shouts. "I'm taking you down personally, you overgrown lizard-bot!"

As Bumblebee moves to gather the rest of his team, the red blip on the radar flickers in and out like a dying lightbulb.

The Autobot leans in closer to examine the screen. The light flickers again, and then a second red light pops into existence a short distance from the first.

"A second Decepticon!" Bumblebee says. "Skinkbomb must have an ally!"

The two lights flicker and blink in unison like a pair of eyes.

"Are they trying to disguise their signals? I've got to get the others and track these two down before they disappear!"

Just then, a loud, familiar voice pipes through the speakers.

"WHY DO YOU FIGHT AGAINST US, BUMBLEBEE?" the voice asks.

Bumblebee recoils from the screen.

An outline appears around the two red lights, bringing Optimus's face into view. The red eyes make the electronic approximation of Bumblebee's former leader look even more sinister.

"JOIN ME, BUMBLEBEE, AND RULE

BY MY SIDE WHEN MY DECEPTICONS SQUASH YOUR PUNY AUTOBOTS."

"Stop this, whoever you are!" Bumblebee yells back at the screen. "I know you're not really Optimus. You're just a Decepticon trick, and Team Bee's specialty is taking you down!"

"TELL THAT TO SIDESWIPE…IF HE RECOVERS!"

Bumblebee pulls back his fist and darts forward to destroy the console.

"Sir, stop!" Strongarm shouts, appearing in the doorway to the command center. "What are you doing?"

The Autobot leader turns around and takes in the concerned faces of Strongarm, Grimlock, Fixit, Rusty, and Denny, all cautiously keeping their distance from him.

"Can't you see?" Bumblebee asks, pointing behind him. "Somebot infected our systems with an evil version of Optimus!"

The teammates look at one another, worried, then frown at their leader.

Bee turns back to the console and sees that the screen displays a normal map, with only one bright red blip in the quarry. The flashing red eyes and clear outline of Optimus's profile are nowhere to be found.

"It…it was here just before you came in," Bumblebee tries to explain. "It was taunting me and threatening our team."

Fixit whispers to Denny and Russell, and the two humans leave the room, a concerned look cast on their faces.

"Bumblebee, perhaps you should let me tick…tock…take a look at your wiring," the Mini-Con says, rolling toward the confused yellow bot. "The negative effects of group management stress are not to be underestimated and can lead to—"

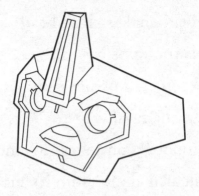

"Wait a minute," Bumblebee interrupts, taking a step back. "Do you all think I'm malfunctioning?"

Strongarm, Grimlock, and Fixit exchange glances.

Grimlock takes a careful step forward, his bulky arms outstretched.

"Let's all calm down, Bee," the Dinobot says, inching toward his leader. "We're all friend-bots here, right?"

Bumblebee shakes his head vigorously, clearing his thoughts.

"Grim, stop it, I'm not going to do anything crazy," he says.

The Dinobot continues to move closer until Strongarm elbows him to cut it out.

"I know what I'm saying sounds unusual, but hear me out. Somebot has been sending me evil visions of Optimus trying to distract me."

"I believe you, sir, but a tune-up never hurt anybot!" Fixit adds, approaching Bumblebee with forced cheerfulness.

"Fixit," Bumblebee says. "I don't have brain rust. I admit I'm shaken up by what happened to Sideswipe, but someone is messing with us, and I intend to put an end to it!"

The other Autobots in the room look at
one another with renewed confidence in their
leader.

"But first we have a Decepticon that deserves some payback," Bumblebee says, pointing at the red blip on the screen. "And as Sideswipe would say, 'What goes around, comes around!'"

Chapter 9

Far away in the Realm of the Primes, a very disgruntled Liege Maximo stomps and kicks at the ground.

"These Autobots are NO FUN AT ALL!" he bellows, blowing up several fake bots.

"All I ask for in this vast, endless existence is some semblance of joy, and these boring bots are intent on keeping that away from me with their 'teamwork' and 'justice' and 'loyalty'! I can taste the fuel coming back up my intake valve!"

Liege Maximo's horns twitch, and a full legion of mindless bots appear before him, covered in all manner of slicing blades, blunt maces, and spiky armor.

"If all those awful Autobots want is some fight to destruction against a grand evil, then I'll give them the destruction they seek!"

"Who is Liege Maximo?" Optimus asks, his frame tensing.

"He's above your pay grade," Micronus explains. "Liege Maximo is one of us, an original Prime and member of the Thirteen. Long, long ago, Liege Maximo grew bored of our existence. He's never been truly evil, but his cruelty and penchant for manipulation are legendary. To relieve his boredom with the power he wields, Liege Maximo uses it to pit brother against brother for his own amusement."

"Brother against brother?" Optimus asks. "Micronus, before you arrived, I was attacked by something that took the shape of my teammate Bumblebee from Earth. It spoke in Bumblebee's voice and looked just like him, but the things he said…"

"That's Liege Maximo's doing, all right," Micronus says. "He is one of us, and we tolerate him, but his lies and treacheries have cost us dearly in the past. Now it looks like he's trying to have some twisted 'fun' with you."

Optimus narrows his optics and pounds his mighty metal fists together.

"If this is Liege Maximo's idea of fun, then it's time we twist it back at him," Optimus says with gusto.

Micronus laughs.

"Optimus, you're not ready for a Prime!" Micronus says. "You'll meet Liege Maximo in time, and he might even teach you a thing or two worth knowing down the line, but this is one problem you can't punch to scrap."

The Autobot leader's tactical brain races with ideas.

"The false Bumblebee's patience didn't last very long when I called it on its bluff," Optimus says. "It seems like Liege Maximo gets bored of his games as soon as they don't go his way. I think we can use that to our advantage."

Micronus smiles. Immensely powerful foe or not, this is one trial that his pupil seems ready to take on.

Back on Earth, Bumblebee leads Strongarm and Grimlock toward Skinkbomb's signal in the quarry. Fixit, Rusty, and Denny stayed back in the scrapyard to take care of Sideswipe. Bumblebee's and Strongarm's wheels tear rivets into the ground, and Grimlock's pounding feet shake the trees around them.

"You know I have utmost faith in you, sir," Strongarm says to the yellow bot speeding ahead of her. "But even if you're not suffering from early symptoms of brain rust, we're still one Autobot short against a Decepticon that nearly turned us into spare parts last time we squared off against him."

"Fixit said Skinkbomb needs to consume large amounts of metal and flammable oils to regrow his tail-bomb. If we can catch up to him before he's eaten enough, we may have an upper hand."

Bumblebee shifts into a higher gear, spitting grass and dirt behind him as he goes.

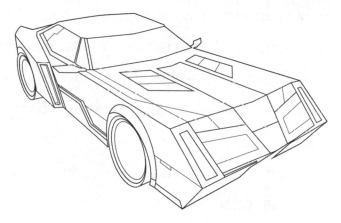

"And this time, I won't be so easily distracted."

Bumblebee, Strongarm, and Grimlock

arrive at the edge of the quarry in good time. The Autobot leader whispers into his wrist communicator.

"We're about to enter the quarry, Fixit. If you have any luck getting in touch with Drift, give him our coordinates."

The bots scan the rocky landscape for any sign of their explosive enemy.

They follow a loud crunching noise around a bend and spot Skinkbomb, chewing on a construction crane and guzzling barrels of oil!

"Autobots, it's time to ignite the dynamite!" Bumblebee yells.

This lame attempt at a catchphrase causes his teammates to roll their optics, but it does catch Skinkbomb's attention.

The three bots charge from their hiding spot.

Bumblebee and Strongarm, still in their vehicle modes, crash into Skinkbomb, knocking him off balance and causing him to spill the oil in his claws.

Grimlock leaps into the air and comes thundering down on the Decepticon, knocking the wind out of his pistons and pinning him to the ground.

"Why don't you try eating my Dino-Destructo Double Drop instead?" the towering Dinobot yells.

"You really think you goody two-treads could take me out that easy?" Skinkbomb asks, struggling under Grimlock's bulk. "Don't you know who I am?"

The Decepticon uses his pinned arm to tap at a button on his side.

A cascade of small spheres pour out of the containers around his waist—microbombs!

"Uh-oh," Grimlock says.

KABOOM-BOOM-BOOM!

A series of explosions ring out around Skinkbomb, the sound and vibrations echoing loudly through the quarry.

Grimlock is thrown backward, allowing

Skinkbomb to pull himself up and run back to the oil drums.

Through the haze of dust and smoke, Bumblebee sees that Skinkbomb's tail is nearly regrown. He has to reach the Decepticon before he can finish his meal!

The yellow Autobot leaps into his bot mode and pulls out his blaster.

Bumblebee lets loose a series of shots that opens up the oil container like swiss cheese.

"Looks like you've sprung a leak, lizard-bot!" Bumblebee cries.

His drink decimated, the aggravated Skinkbomb hurls the rapidly emptying drum at Bumblebee's head.

The Autobot leader ducks a nanocycle too late and catches the corner of the barrel. The force of the impact knocks him off his treads, and he lands facedown in a pool of spilled oil.

Bumblebee quickly scrambles to his feet, but not before catching his reflection in the oil—and watching it quickly turn into the sinister, grinning face of Optimus!

Chapter 10

Liege Maximo looks down into the portal to Earth, crowing in delight as he summons an evil Optimus vision to taunt Bumblebee during battle.

"Oh, is the little Autobot distracted by his big, bad friend?"

Micronus suddenly appears behind the fiendish trickster.

"Sticking your horns where they don't belong, Liege Maximo?"

The mischief-maker leaps up in shock, preparing to blast Micronus.

"Let's not bother with the knuckle dusting," Micronus says, hovering confidently in front of the horned bot. "We both know we're too evenly matched for it to amount to anything but a waste of time."

Liege Maximo's optics flare with anger.

"Time is all we have, Micronus! Don't you see how infinitely boring this realm has become? Manipulating these inconsequential Autobots is my new favorite pastime."

"Your 'fun' is done, trickster!"

Liege Maximo's horns twitch.

He makes a grand gesture with his hands and a smile cracks across his face.

"On the contrary, Micronus. My fun is NOT done.…It has just begun!"

Back on Earth, Bumblebee pulls himself

up from the puddle of oil. Optimus's eerie face isn't a trick of the light—it's staring up at the Autobot leader with hatred in its optics.

"BUMBLEBEE," the voice echoes through the canyon. "YOU'RE A FOOL TO STAND AGAINST US. YOUR TEAM WILL FALL ONE BY ONE—JUST LIKE THE BOT YOU ALREADY FAILED."

Skinkbomb, Grimlock, and Strongarm

look around to see the source of the booming voice.

"Sir, why does that voice sound like Optimus?" Strongarm asks, drawing her blaster into a ready-to-fire position.

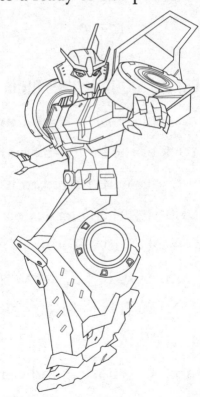

"Whoa," Grimlock says. "Maybe we've *all* got brain rust!"

"No, Grim, this is nothing more than a trick," Bumblebee says. "Is this your doing, Decepticon?"

Skinkbomb takes advantage of the confusion to scurry back to the oil drums.

"I'm not responsible for this spooky stereo act, but I sure enjoy dinner and a show!" The Decepticon begins shoveling metal scraps and great gulps of oil into his wide maw.

"You're going on a diet, Skinkbomb!" Bumblebee shouts. "Grimlock, clean his plate for him!"

Grimlock nods and transforms into his Tyrannosaurus rex mode. The brutish bot smashes his tail into the ground, creating a shockwave that sends the remaining oil cans rolling across the quarry floor. With another wide swing of his tail, Grimlock swats the metal out of Skinkbomb's claws.

"Strongarm, let's defuse this explosive situation!" Bee says.

The law-bot leaps onto Skinkbomb's back,

pinning the Decepticon's arms. Bumblebee dashes over and grabs hold of the nearly complete ticking time bomb of a tail.

"GIVE UP, BUMBLEBEE!" the imposter Optimus shouts. "WE DECEPTICONS ARE LEGION. YOU CANNOT DEFEAT US ALL!"

"I might not be able to defeat you all by myself," Bumblebee says, tugging on the tail bomb. "But luckily—I don't have to!"

Grimlock, back in bot mode, grabs hold alongside Bumblebee. With Strongarm keeping Skinkbomb's arms bound, Bumblebee and Grimlock succeed in pulling the criminal's incendiary tail loose!

"TOO LATE, AUTOBOT FOOLS!" the voice booms.

Bumblebee looks at the tail bomb in his hands. It's ticking!

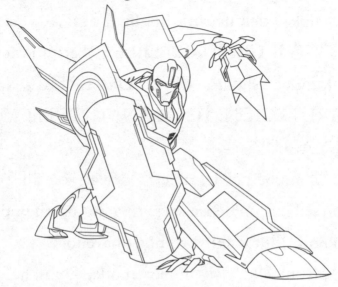

"Autobots, burn rubber!"

Bumblebee throws the bomb over his shoulder, and the three bots rush away with their captive in tow. They make it to the edge of the quarry before the force from the explosion knocks them flat.

KRAKA-BOOOOOM!

Bumblebee, Grimlock, and Strongarm stumble to their treads, their audio receptors still ringing.

Skinkbomb tries to scurry into the surrounding forest, but Grimlock quickly nabs the slippery lizardbot in an iron grip.

"It's going to take more than a cheap imitation of Optimus and a few firecrackers to defeat this team!" Bumblebee says proudly.

In the Realm of the Primes, Optimus waits and meditates.

When his mentor, Micronus, left to confront Liege Maximo, he warned Optimus to prepare for an attack.

I have learned much during these simulated exercises, Optimus thinks to himself. *I may need more time and training before I'm prepared to face off against this impending evil, but I'm ready right now for any child's play that Liege Maximo can conjure up!*

A fog begins to roll across the ground, carrying with it ominous cries from all directions:

"Earth has fallen!"

"Bumblebee betrayed us all!"

"How could the Autobots abandon us like this?"

The red-and-blue Autobot leader climbs to his feet and calmly draws his sword. He speaks evenly into the void, no trace of emotion in his voice.

"Your tricks and taunts don't bother me, Liege Maximo. They never did."

Optimus's optics scan the fog.

Several figures appear in the distance, rapidly making their way toward his position. Malicious mockeries of Bumblebee, Strongarm, Grimlock, Sideswipe, and Fixit leap out of the fog and attack Optimus!

Optimus carves his blade in a wide arc, slashing through his attackers without hesitation.

WHOOSH!

Five of the six false Autobots fall to the ground and shatter into fragments of quickly disappearing light.

SKEESH!

Only the evil Bumblebee remains.

"Your confidence in these bots is misplaced, Optimus," Bumblebee says. "They will let you down. They are weak and easily manipulated!"

"I don't think so, Liege Maximo," Optimus replies. "Bumblebee and the other bots are the bravest, most trustworthy bots I know.

The only weak and easily manipulated one I see around here is *you*."

Before Bumblebee can respond, Optimus steps forward and drives his blade through the illusion, sending it scattering into flickers of light.

FWISSSS!

"Curses! It's not fair! It's not—" an angry voice echoes through the Realm before being abruptly cut off.

When Optimus turns around, Micronus is hovering before him once more.

"You done good, kid," Micronus says, a grin plastered to his face.

"Has Liege Maximo been defeated?" Optimus asks.

"It's not as simple as that. Liege Maximo

might be a menace, but he is one of us. The Primes will find a way to punish him, though. I promise you that."

"And his tricks?"

"Over for now," Micronus says. "And even if he tried again, you and Bumblebee are too wise for him."

"Bumblebee?" Optimus asks. "Did Liege

Maximo involve the real Bumblebee in all of this?"

"Oh yeah, I forgot to mention—that wily wreck of a Prime was tinkering with your pal on Earth in the same way. Confused him for a nanocycle or two, but Bumblebee shook it off just as quickly as you did. Seems he isn't too shabby of a leader himself."

Optimus beams with pride for his former lieutenant.

"You might want to give him a few words of encouragement, though," Micronus says. "Never hurts to hear a kind word from a friend."

He waves his hands and opens a portal to the scrapyard. Bumblebee and the other bots are gathered around Fixit's repair table.

Sideswipe picks himself up, clutching at his injured back with a grimace.

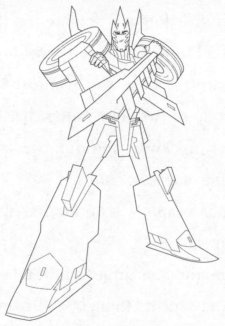

"Solus knows I could sure use a buff job!" he quips.

Team Bee feels a wash of relief that their friend and teammate is almost back to normal.

"Don't rush your repair phase, Sideswipe," Bumblebee says, gently pushing the younger bot back down to the table. "I think your heroism earned you a few cycles of rest mode."

"What would you do without me, Bee?" Sideswipe asks.

"Let's not answer that," Bumblebee says with a laugh.

With Skinkbomb safely deposited in a stasis pod and Sideswipe's prognosis looking better, the bots are looking forward to a little downtime.

Suddenly, their brief peace is interrupted by a much-too-familiar voice booming through the audio system.

"BUMBLEBEE!"

"Oh no, not this again!" Bumblebee says.

He pulls his blaster and aims it at the screen where Optimus's face has materialized.

"This is no trick, Bee," Optimus explains.

Bumblebee cautiously lowers his weapon.

"...Optimus?"

"I wish I could explain everything to you, but I can't. With time, I will. But what I can tell you is that you're a wise, worthy leader—and a fantastic friend."

"I knew it couldn't be you, Optimus," Bumblebee says. "There's no one I trust more on Earth, Cybertron, or wherever you are now."

The other bots look on with smiles as their leader reconnects with his mentor.

"I'm being tested in the Realm of the Primes, Bumblebee," Optimus states. "And I think you and I just passed an unexpected pair of trials. So, in a way, we were fighting side by side like the good old days. I'm grateful that Earth is under the watch of a confident, clear-headed Autobot like you, Bumblebee. You and your team have made me proud."

Bumblebee stands tall with his friends beaming around him.

As quickly as it appeared, the vision of Optimus begins to fade.

"And in some time soon," Optimus says, "I'll be proud to protect Earth alongside you once again!"